# No More Time

# NO MORE TIME

## Selected Stories

CARMINE PARI

Published by Redequal Publishing
ISBN: 0692460799
ISBN 13: 9780692460795

# DEDICATION

I dedicate this book to its readers,
those who have allowed me to share
my art, a piece of myself, with them.

To be or not to be, that is the question—
Whether 'tis nobler in the mind to suffer
The slings and arrows of outrageous fortune,
Or to take arms against a sea of troubles
And by opposing, end them. To die, to sleep—
No more—and by a sleep to say we end
The heartache and the thousand natural shocks
That flesh is heir to—'tis a consummation
Devoutly to be wished. To die, to sleep,
To sleep, perchance to dream.

William Shakespeare

# Author's Note

# CONTENT

# A SCARY STORY

WE WERE THE only ones sitting at the bar. I was sitting to his left. He drank with his left. I could see his watch. Rolex.

"Nick," he said to the bartender, "get my friend here a drink."

"No, thank you," I said. "I'm just having a beer."

"It's on me."

Nick came over.

"Same thing," the man told him.

Nick grabbed the MACALLAN 25 and began pouring it into a glass.

"Make it a double," the man told him after the pour.

"That's good," I said. The drink was already a double.

The man jerked up his shoulders and smirked, seeming to say it was my loss.

Nick handed me the glass and left.

"Thanks," I said to my new friend, making sure not to add that I would get the next round, and sipped the whisky.

My new friend turned to me. "So, what's your name?"

The light overhead highlighted his tanned face in the otherwise sallow and concealing gloom of the bar.

"Daniel," I said. "Daniel Portsman."

"Portsman. Portsman," he repeated. "Sounds like a good name. Are you a good name?"

He slurred his words ever so slightly.

"Most of the time," I said, taking a swig of my drink. I licked my teeth. The whisky was worth the money.

"Mike Glover," the man said, now looking back toward the mirror and lines of bottles behind the restaurant's bar.

I assumed that was his name.

"What dragged you to Ruth's?" he asked.

The time was a little after nine on a Wednesday evening in Woodland Hills, a quiet city in the San Fernando Valley, and I didn't want to be alone in my townhouse. I had no date or friends to hang out with for the evening. The dull atmosphere of Ruth Chris's Steakhouse bar seemed appropriate for how I was feeling.

"Boredom," I answered.

"A good reason," he said. "The best reason. Boredom is sometimes welcomed company."

I tilted my head a little to the side. I wasn't sure what he meant. My growing buzz rejected any desire to contemplate the statement.

He nodded gently. "Cheers," he said.

We drank. His drink disappeared down his gullet. Mine barely lowered; I wanted to relish it.

He raised a hand to get Nick's attention.

Nick poured him another double.

"You want another?" Mike asked me.

I held out my glass. The whisky was half finished. "I'm good."

"Pour him a standby," he told Nick.

Nick did and placed the glass on a napkin in front of me.

With the fingers of both hands, Mike spun his glass slowly on the bar.

"So what's your story?" he asked me.

"I don't have a story," I said.

"Everyone has a story."

"Well, I don't have one."

"Tell me one anyway." He said with authority, as if he were used to giving orders and having people follow them.

My head jerked back. "A story?"

"Something meaningful...or interesting."

"What do you mean?"

"It's early," he said. "I'm going to be here for a while. You tell the stories. I'll buy the drinks."

Knowing the whisky was outrageously expensive, I said "Sure," and downed the remainder of my first drink.

"Any scary? You have any scary stories?" he asked me.

I thought about it. The time I swam out into the ocean at three in the morning in Cancun to save a screaming woman came to mind. Fighting nine men aiming to hurt me in a fast food restaurant in Palmdale struck me. But the young man outside a 7-Eleven in Tarzana at one in the afternoon was the scariest story I could think of at that moment.

"I have some stories. A couple," I said.

"Just a couple?" he asked.

"How many should I have?"

"How old are you, son?"

"Thirty."

"You're young. At my age, one has many stories."

He appeared to be thinking about what to say next. I didn't speak.

"We make sense of what we experience by creating stories. We remember our lives with stories. Our memories are stories," he finally said.

I nodded. He might have seen me through the corner of his eye, but he looked to be focused on his glass.

"Everyone has stories to tell," he continued. "The older one is, the more one has."

He turned and looked straight into my eyes. I felt uncomfortable, as if he knew something about me that even I didn't know.

"You have more," he said. "We all do. We all have stories to tell. People are storytellers. That's what we are, storytellers."

I supposed the whisky was loosening his lips.

He sipped his whisky and turned back to face the mirror behind the bar, appearing to study his reflection: his short, silver hair, sitting on his golden-toned skin. I supposed we all scrutinize ourselves in bar mirrors.

I noticed my white skin and brown hair contrasted with his. We could have been a father and son just having a drink together.

"I'm not much of a storyteller," I told my stout and handsome friend.

"Everyone is a storyteller. Everyone has a story to tell."

He turned and studied me. I felt inadequate in my slacks and dress shirt. His suit was a fine gray material. His button shirt was white. He wore no tie.

My buzz was growing. My tongue felt freer. And despite my reluctance, I began my story.

"It was three summers ago," I began. "I pulled up in front of a convenience store in Tarzana."

I stopped talking to determine if my friend was listening.

"Go on," he said, as if he detected my hesitation, my uneasiness and discomfort. I felt like I was on a job interview, answering a question interviewing managers often ask: Tell me of a time when you handled a difficult situation with a client.

I continued my story. "I saw a young man sitting in front of the store, his back resting against the glass several feet from the entrance. His head was bent down, so I couldn't see his face behind his sandy-colored hair. I had seen many homeless and druggies at convenience stores over the years, often at this very store. But there was something about this man's posture that struck me as I looked at him through my windshield. As I said, he was sitting against the glass wall with his head bent over, but he wasn't sitting up straight. Let me see if I can describe his posture in words. His butt was away from the wall, so that his back was leaning against it at a forty-five degree angle. His feet were out in front of him with his knees bent. His wrists were on his knees, and his hands hung loosely. He looked dejected, spent, as if he had given up. The image of Christ came to mind. I don't know why. Maybe my Catholic guilt or my desire to show more Christian charity than I could afford."

I paused to take a sip of my *standby* whisky.

"It's a good story," Mike said, nodding his head. "I like it so far."

Hmm, I thought, raising my eyebrows and turning my upper lip down a bit.

Where was I, I thought.

"I got out of my car and walked to the double-door entrance. I expected the usual: the young man to look up at me, to ask if I could spare some change, to do and ask what all beggars that I have encountered hanging out in front of convenience stores have done, yet at the same time I wasn't surprised when he just looked up at me for a moment and returned his head to its hanging position, facing the ground."

I stopped again to see if Mike was following along, to see if my story was making sense to him.

"You want to hear more?" I asked him.

He didn't look at me. He was looking down at his drink. "Go on."

I nodded, though I wasn't sure he even saw me do it.

"I felt pity for the young man. At least that's what I thought I was feeling. It's hard to really describe the feeling with one word, or even several. My emotions were stirring. I *wanted* to help him. 'Are you hungry,' I asked him, knowing the answer just had to be *yes*. He looked up at me, again. He appeared to have no emotion in his face, no anger, no regret or remorse or pain or ... He had given up. I knew it. I sensed it. There was no fight left in him. He would take what the world would give him without complaint or expectation."

I was feeling loose now, feeling friendly and talkative. I was in a groove. I wanted to tell my story. And I wanted someone to hear it, to listen to it, to understand it, understand me.

I took a good swig of my drink. It was tasting better now, vanilla and honey notes.

"Thanks for the drink," I said to Mike.

He smiled, but still he didn't look up. I just saw the left corner of his mouth turn up, his cheek bulge a bit, and the small wrinkles on the side of his eye get a little deeper.

"It's a good story so far," is what he said.

I let out an audible breath and continued my story.

"As I said, the young man just looked up at me and said, 'Yes.' He had an attractive face.

"'Come on,' I said. 'Let's get you something to eat.' The lean man got up and followed me into the store. I walked to the grill that had hotdogs cooking.

"'Would you like a couple of hotdogs?' I asked him, thinking he would welcome a hot meal, or at least a warm one. 'Do you even eat hotdogs?' I asked him.

"'Yeah!' he said, with a little spirit. It's amazing what a little food can do for the soul.

"'Get yourself whatever you want to drink,' I told him. 'No booze, though.' I bunned the dogs, and he went to the refrigerators and picked out some ice tea. I asked him what he wanted on the dogs when he came back.

"'Everything,' he said. No surprise there. I handed him the cardboard holder with the dogs and took the tea. He loaded them up: gobs of onion and relish. Then I told him to get whatever food he wanted.

"'What?' he responded.

"'Get whatever you need: cereal, bread, milk, whatever.'

"'You sure?' he asked me. I wasn't expecting that. I thought he would have rushed to the shelves and begun pilling goods into his arms. I directed him to put the dogs on the counter. I handed him a plastic hand basket and again told him to get what he needed. He was hesitant. I walked down the aisle, and he followed. I grabbed different items and asked him if he wanted them. We got cereal, bread, milk, cookies; cans of beans, tuna, corned beef hash, and I can't remember what else. I brought the basket up to the counter and brought him back another one. I made sure he filled the second one as well."

Mike turned to me. I didn't know what to expect. Did he hear enough? Did he want me to stop, change to another story? I felt anxious. I didn't want to disappoint him; we were drinking MACALLAN 25 after all.

He pulled his lips in tight and furrowed his brow a bit, looking to be thinking hard.

I waited.

"Daniel, aye? Daniel Portsman?"

I hesitated for a moment. "Yes, sir."

"A good name," he said, and waived Nick over to refill his drink.

"Give us another," Mike told Nick.

My drink was dented but not totaled. I downed it. Seconds later, we had clean glasses and liquid comfort swaying in them.

Mike reached into his pocket and placed a rectangular key fob on the bar, a Bentley key fob with its iconic B and silver wings. My forehead wrinkled with surprise.

"I'll be back in a minute," he said, and walked off.

Nick was wiping off the bar with a towel. He saw the fob, but I didn't notice a reaction of surprise from him.

"Do you know Mike?" I asked him.

He stopped wiping and looked at me. "Mr. Glover. He owns Glover Jet."

I had heard of the business jet manufacturer. All kinds of news about his company had been on news stations and the internet, something about offshore funds and banking.

"That's him?" I asked.

He pointed to the fob. "The other half of that is parked in two spaces out back with our parking attendants."

I nodded.

"Is he always this friendly?" I asked.

"He's a nice guy. Lost his son last year. It was in the news. Drugs. Don't mention it to him. He's my best customer."

I shook my head. "Sure thing."

I sipped my drink.

Ten minutes later Mike returned to his seat. I stood. He was a couple of inches taller than me; six two I guessed.

"Sorry to interrupt your story. Where were you?"

We sat back on the stools.

"Continue, please," Mike said.

I nodded and continued my story.

"The cashier bagged the food and I paid for it. The young man carried the two bags and I carried the hotdogs. I opened the door for him. He walked over to the side of the building. I followed him. He placed the bags down and sat on the low wall. I handed him the hotdogs. I thought he would devour them like a hungry wolf, but he didn't. He took his time, appearing to meditate on the taste. He closed his eyes as he chewed. 'Thanks, man,' he said. I assumed he was referring to me.

"'Are you okay," I asked. It was a stupid question, but I didn't know what else to say. I was ashamed, ashamed of myself, ashamed of what I was, what I was a part of. He nodded his head and grinned. I reached into my pocket and counted out my bills. 'Take this,' I said and handed him all I had. The money would feed him for a week or two, I thought. He didn't look like a druggie. He didn't really look homeless. He was a good-looking kid just down on his luck.

"He took the bills slowly. 'Thanks, man.' I was sure he was thanking me that time. I just watched him for a few minutes.

"'I have to get going,' I finally said. He smiled and nodded as if he knew I had done all I was capable of doing. 'Take care,' I said and returned to my car."

Then a thought hit me: I was feeling the same way about Mike as I had about that young man at the 7-Eleven. Or at least I thought I was. I wasn't sure. The whisky was having its effect on me: intensifying my emotions and confusing me somewhat.

I drank a nip and continued. "As I drove away, the tears rose in my eyes. I wanted to help the young man, but when I thought about what I had done, I realized I had failed. I didn't really help him. At best, I prolonged his pain for a while. I gave him the energy and time to think about and find a back alley to rest in or a tree beside a freeway to sleep under. I helped give him the physical energy to do the same thing the following day, to repeat his desperate situation. What would change for him the next day, the next week? Thinking about it pained me because I knew the answer. Nothing would change for him. Nothing would change for him until someone *really* helped him. I mean helped him get a roof over his head, a bed to sleep in, a job, the ability to earn money to survive, to have friends, possibly a family, to be human. I didn't help him. I was scared. I knew that man could be me. That man was me, all of us. More tears flowed."

I swirled the whisky in my glass for a minute. "That's my story," I said to Mike.

He turned to look at me. He stared into my eyes. I was okay with it. He reached out his right hand. I shook it while he did the same.

"That is a scary story, Daniel," he said, "an honest-to-goodness scary story."

I raised my eyebrows. "And it's a true story."

"I have no doubt it is," he said, "no doubt at all."

He reached into his pocket and took out a business card, a Glover Jet business card, and gave it to me.

"If you ever need anything, you call me," he said. "If you ever need a job or are down on *your* luck, you call me."

I stared at the card.

"I won't forget your story, Daniel. Do you understand?"

"Yes," I said, but I didn't understand.

He checked the air with his thumb and forefinger as Nick looked over at us. After he signed the credit card receipt, he placed three hundred-dollar bills on the bar for a tip.

Then he did something unexpected, almost weird really. He unclasped his Rolex, a gold Rolex, and handed it to me.

"Take care of this for me," he said. "It needs a lot of wearing."

I was dumbfounded and buzzed. And I'm sure the expression on my face wasn't one of intelligence: mouth open and eyes wide.

He turned and walked away before I could speak.

Thinking he would come back, I stood looking toward the entrance into the bar. For a minute I waited, but he didn't return. Finally, I sat and thought about my new story while I finished my drink.

I wear the watch every day.

# THE SAMARITAN OF
# PINE MOUNTAIN

AS HE STEERED along the dark country road, he saw the red taillights about two hundred yards ahead of him rise and turn clockwise as the vehicle began to roll. Gold sparks shot out from it as it overturned onto its roof and scraped against the pavement. Gripping the steering wheel with both hands and flooring the accelerator, he sped toward the flipped vehicle. As he closed in on it, he could see it had launched off the side of the road and crashed into a field of shrubs and bushes. Fortunately, few trees grew along this section of road, which headed into Pine Mountain.

He stopped just where the vehicle had slid off the road—where gray scrapes showed on the black pavement, and plumes of dirt and dust, kicked up by the abrading vehicle, filled the air—and pointed his headlights toward the field. He shut off the engine and jumped out of his car. Hearing no one, he dashed toward the vehicle.

"Is anyone hurt?" he hollered, his heart thumping. "Are you okay? Anyone?"

Scrambling through the sand and vegetation, he reached a black sport utility vehicle. It lay in a ditch, with the passenger side facing up and the door open. Its engine and lights were dead, but his car's headlights provided some light. He peered into the vehicle and saw someone moving. He couldn't discern whether the person was a man or a woman, or how many people were inside the cabin. Then he heard moaning.

"Are you all right?" he asked. There was no answer, just the sound of clambering. "You shouldn't move," he warned. Silence. Then someone began crawling up toward him.

"Here, give me your hand," he said, and reached into the vehicle. A hand stretched out and grabbed his. Seeing the slender fingers, he realized the person was a woman. He pulled her up gradually as she groaned and struggled to climb out. She was blond, with an attractive face and firm body. Early thirties, he guessed. He lowered her from the side panel and helped her lean against the vehicle's roof. Gasping and holding her left abdomen, she was obviously in pain. Glistening blood covered much of the left side of her blouse and skirt.

"Are you alone?" he asked, crouching in front of her. "Was anyone else with you? A baby? A child?"

Head down and wobbling, she appeared not to hear him, so he climbed back to the open door and double-checked the cabin. No one was inside. Still not satisfied, he scanned the ground around the vehicle but saw and heard no one.

He turned his attention back to the woman. "Can you hear me?" he asked, speaking loudly and emphasizing every word.

"Yes," she finally said, nodding her head.

"Were you alone?" he asked again.

"Yes...alone," she murmured.

She grimaced in agony and pressed her hands on her belly. She clearly needed a hospital—and quickly.

Then dread hit him as he recalled where they were. The road leading to the mountain was long and desolate, and the nearest town was miles away. "Lie still. You'll be okay. Just lie still," he told her and thought, *I'll call the...*

Then he remembered his cell phone didn't work in this area and that the chance of a car driving by was slim. There were only two homes on this road, and the time was after 1:00 a.m. *No help is coming*, he realized. But he didn't panic.

"Do you have a cell phone?" he asked, thinking another phone might get a signal.

"No," she said.

He thought quickly. *Check her injuries, stop the bleeding, get her into my car, drive her to town where my cell phone will work. Then emergency services can get an ambulance out to meet us or tell me where to take her. Or should I leave her here and go get help? What if she bleeds to death?*

"I need to see how badly you're bleeding...check your wounds," he told her. "Is that okay?"

She nodded, and he immediately knelt and lifted her bloodied white blouse. Sticky blood covered her pale skin, and blood oozed from a dark hole in her side. For a moment, he felt dizzy.

Thinking quickly, he ran back to his car and popped the trunk lid with the remote. From a gym bag he pulled out a white towel, and from the corner he grabbed a sweater. He slammed the lid and rushed back to her.

"We'll have to hold this to your side to stop the bleeding," he said, and set the folded towel over her wound. Then he folded his sweater and positioned it over the towel. "Hold this here," he told her as he took her left hand and placed it over the sweater. She took in a quick breath and groaned. He stopped for a moment.

"I'm…okay," she faltered.

He drew her gently away from the roof, wrapped the arms of the sweater around her waist, and tied the sleeves atop the towel on her left side.

"My purse…I need my purse," she whispered.

"You need your purse?"

"My medicine."

He placed her delicately back against the vehicle and climbed into it. A minute later, he found the purse and hastened it to her.

"Here it is," he said.

She reached for it slowly, gasping.

"Would you like me to look for you?" he asked, kneeling next to her.

She didn't answer but rummaged through the purse and pulled out a silver box, about the size of an eyeglass case. In the light from his car's headlights, he saw her open the box, retrieve a dark pill and place it into her mouth. Then she removed a small cylinder, which looked like a short pen. She held one end of it against her left forearm. *Some kind of injection*, he thought. She swallowed hard, closed her eyes, and sat back again.

"We need to get you some help," he told her. "I'm going to get you into my car, and we're going to find a hospital. Understand?"

"Okay," she murmured.

"I'd rather not move you, but my cell phone won't work here," he said nervously. Sweat was dripping from her forehead. He saw the concern in her eyes. *She's in shock, or soon will be*, he thought.

"I'll be okay," she told him, forming a faint smile.

"Of course you will. You'll be in good hands in no time," he said, patting her hand gently. But he didn't believe it. He guessed driving her to an emergency room in town would take at least twenty-five minutes.

"Do you think you can walk?"

She nodded yes.

"Let's go. I'll help you," he said, and carefully tried to lift her.

She cried out, "No, I can't! Something's wrong!"

He didn't hesitate but reached under her and lifted her into his arms. She moaned, but he didn't stop. They had already wasted valuable time, and he thought she might die if he waited any longer. Pumped with adrenaline, he practically ran with her.

He reached the passenger side of his vehicle and, still holding her, managed to grab the handle and open the door. In seconds, he buckled her into the seat, then dashed around the front of the car, jumped in, jammed the key in the ignition, and sped off. "Hold tight," he said. But she only held tight to her blood-soaked compress.

He was flying back the way they had come when—

"Not this way," she said. "You must take me up the mountain."

"What? The town is this way. You need a hospital."

"Please, you must trust me. Turn around!" she said, panicking.

"Listen. You need a doctor. It won't take long to get to—"

"Turn around. Please!" She began to sob. "I'll *die* if you don't."

"You'll die if I *do*. Besides, I don't want to go to jail because I didn't take you to a damned hospital. They have these Good Samaritan laws, you know."

"I know it's hard for you to understand," she said, controlling her sobbing. "But the help I need is on the mountain."

"You need a hospital. I don't know what you landed on, but that injury is bad."

"I didn't land on anything," she said. "I've been shot."

He slammed on the brakes and looked at her, his eyes wide and mouth agape. Confused, and scared, he felt his blood drain from his face.

"What in *hell* is going on? Is that why you crashed? Someone shot you from the side of the road?"

"No," she said. "I was shot before I got into my truck. I was on my way to get help when I blacked out."

"Am I in danger?"

"No."

"Are you sure?"

"You're in no danger."

He thought about asking more questions but decided minding his own business and focusing on the current danger—to her life—was safer.

"Listen, I live at the base of that mountain, and there's only one other house besides mine on the entire road. The only help you'll get is in town, and I think we should hurry."

"I took medications. I'll be okay for a while, but I must get to the mountain."

"No offense, but I think you banged your head a little too hard. You're going to need more than an aspirin. You're in shock."

She didn't reply.

Miles ahead he could see the town's lights glistening. "I promise I can have you in a hospital in no time. The town is only about twelve miles away."

She was staring at him, pleading with her eyes. Then she opened her purse and pulled out what looked like a cell phone. She touched some icons on its screen.

"Hey, you told me you didn't have a cell phone!" he said.

"This isn't a cell phone," she said, keeping her eyes on the device. Then she touched more icons and placed the gadget against her left forearm. Again she studied the glowing screen.

"You must get me to the mountain," she said. "I don't have much time. The medications I took will wear off soon. You must hurry. Please!"

"I told you...I'm taking you to a hospital."

"Please. *I'll die!* You'll understand when we get to the mountain. I swear."

Straining to remain calm, he inhaled deeply and sighed. He looked at her. She didn't seem crazy, but maybe she wasn't thinking straight. *Possibly a concussion*, he thought, *or shock.*

"I must be the one who's crazy," he said, turning the steering wheel sharply toward the mountain and stomping on the gas. She looked at him silently. He expected at least a thank you, but she said nothing. The car raced at about sixty-five miles per hour along the dark road.

"Okay, where're we going?" he asked.

"Keep going. I'll tell you when we get there," she said.

"Get there! Get where? I told you there's nothing up there."

"My friends are waiting for me."

"Your friends?" Now he really got nervous. *Did she just rob someone? Did she kill anyone? Is she involved in drug dealing?* And the most chilling thought: *Will her friends kill me?* He wanted to turn around and head for town, to get out of this predicament as quickly as possible.

"Listen," she said, "you're worried about not taking me to town, so I have an idea. If anyone questions you, say I held you at gunpoint and forced you to take me up the mountain."

His head snapped back. "So now you're going to pull out a gun and point it at me?" Fear gripped him. *Don't say yes. Please, don't say yes.*

"I don't have a gun."

He lowered his face and turned slightly toward her, giving her a doubtful look: his eyebrows lifted and forehead wrinkled.

"I don't," she said.

"You know what I always say about doing good deeds?" He paused. "Good deeds can become big mistakes. Sometimes we're punished for doing them. I don't want this to be one of those times."

She smiled at him. *With all that blood and in all that pain, she actually smiled.*

"This won't be one of those times," she said.

"I hope not," he said, smiling back.

They were nearing the mountain's base, which was about five miles away from the accident.

"How far up?" he asked.

"Go another five minutes. I'll tell you when to stop."

His house was only three miles ahead, and he regretted he had told her he lived there. With only two houses on the entire road, finding him wouldn't be difficult for her—or her friends. *But she doesn't know my name*, he thought. They hadn't exchanged names, and he hoped she would remember he didn't know hers. The less he knew about her, the better off he thought he was.

The night sky was overcast, and at the base of the mountain, a light fog had formed. The engine raced, as did his pulse. He knew this part of the road well, so he didn't slow down much for the haze.

She said nothing but held the sweater and towel against her side. She grimaced in pain a few times, and that made him even more anxious.

They came to the small gravel road on the right that led up to his house, set roughly seventy-five yards off the main road. He gazed at his entrance as they sped by it. He rarely drove past his house and into the mountain, and doing so now caused him to feel lonely, somehow abandoned.

They continued in silence for about a mile.

"Is it coming up soon?" he asked.

"A couple of minutes more," she said. They were travel-ing about forty miles per hour along the winding road. There was no moonlight, and the tall trees on both sides of the road formed large black barriers that the headlights distorted into strange shapes and gray shadows.

His breathing began to quicken. *This was a big mistake*, he thought. *Foolish. Her friends. Trouble. A lawsuit. Jail time!*

"Pull to the right about a hundred yards ahead," she said. "You'll see a dirt road to your right. Don't turn onto it. Just pull over to the roadside."

He slowed the car and saw the opening in the trees. As he braked to a stop, she looked down at the device in her hand. "We're here," she said.

He shifted into park and kept the engine running.

"There's no one here," he said.

"They're here," she said. "Turn off your engine and lights."

He felt a sudden chill. He didn't want the lights off. He want-ed to see her friends coming, see how many they were. And what if he needed to get away quickly? He wanted the engine running.

"Please," she added. "There's no need to worry."

*Yeah, right*, he thought.

Reluctantly he cut off the headlights. The night was moon-less and black. He killed the engine. Silence. All was still. Neither spoke.

Then out of the darkness, a blue-glowing orb appeared about a hundred feet up the dirt road. This basketball-sized light, centered between the trees, pulsated several yards above the ground.

"*What in the world is that?*" he asked.

"It's just to let you know I won't be alone here."

"Are you sure about this?" he asked.

"Good-bye, and thank you for your help," she said. "And please, tell no one about this. Will you?" she asked, gazing directly at him, studying his face, and holding her device up and pointed at him.

"No. I won't tell anyone…" He paused. "Unless I have to."

She looked at the device's screen. "You are a truthful man."

"That thing tells you that?"

"This…and your face," she told him.

Then she put the device back into her purse and fumbled to open the door.

"I'll help you get out," he said, and opened his door. The cabin lights came on, and the ignition key warning dinged. He stepped out and shut the door. All was dark and quiet. He rushed around to the passenger door and opened it. The cabin again lighted. He helped her onto her feet. She was shaky, so he held her. "Are you sure you'll be all right?" he asked.

"Yes. I'll be fine," she told him. "But you must go now."

He didn't want to go. His anxiety had blended with curiosity. *What kind of friends does she have?*

She gently pushed him back. "Go now. You must."

"Are you sure?"

"Yes," she said. "I'm running out of time."

He closed the passenger door and walked around to the driver's side, where he gave her one last look in the darkness. Slowly he climbed back into the car and closed the door. He started the engine. The interior lights went off. It was dark again. He turned on the headlights and looked out the right side window. She was gone—and so was the blue light.

He turned the car around carefully, gave another look, saw nothing, and started back down the mountain road. He could relax. He was safe.

He drove cautiously and, reaching the gravel road, turned left to his house. The headlights shined off the front windows, which faced the main road. As he continued up the stone driveway to the right, the floodlights on the roof came on. He stopped and turned off the ignition. He thought the house looked lonesome.

A ring startled him. And another ring. It was his cell phone. *But that's not possible*, he thought. It had never worked here; there was no coverage—no signal. But it was ringing. He took it from the tray next to the gearshift and looked at the display. *Unknown caller*— no number. He touched the answer icon and held the phone to his ear. "Hello," he said. There was no sound, no one on the other end. The phone was malfunctioning, he thought. No call was coming in. Then he heard a voice.

"I'm okay now," it said.

He gasped and froze, as if his head had been doused with ice water. He strained to gain his composure, to move, to think. "*Who is this?*" he asked.

A couple of seconds passed, but they felt like minutes.

"Mr. Mason, it's me."

He jerked, then sat straight up in the seat. Whipping his head from side to side, he peered out all the windows. "*Who are you?*" he demanded.

He held his breath, listening, waiting for an answer. It didn't come. The connection was dead. He threw the phone into the tray and started the car. Breathing hard, he backed up quickly, turned the car around, shifted into drive, and tore back down the driveway in a spray of gravel.

Distraught, he raced down the mountain road. His thoughts raced also. *How did she know my number? My name? How did a signal get to my phone?* He wanted to call a friend, anyone. He grabbed his phone and checked it: *No signal.* "Damn!" he yelled, slamming his hand on the wheel. "What the hell is going on!"

He looked in his rear view mirror, expecting to see headlights. He saw black—only black. No one appeared to be following him—in a car, anyway.

He sped on for a few miles until he saw them: *flashing blue lights.* They were about a mile ahead. He thought his heart had stopped. A moment later, he realized they flashed from a police car, that an officer must have found the flipped vehicle. Not wanting to attract attention, he slowed down. Passing the accident, he saw *Sheriff* on the side of the black and white car. Standing just off the road, an officer was scanning the field with his flashlight but turned to look at the passing car.

*Did he see me? My car make? Plate number?* Then he wondered if he should turn around and go tell the officer what had happened. But questions the police might ask rushed to mind: *Why didn't you take her to the hospital? Did you kill her? Where's the body?*

So he did the right thing, what he had given his word to do—not to tell—and kept on driving.

# SILVER DOLPHIN

A LONE IN HIS car, he drove along Topanga Boulevard toward the coast. Once there, he turned left and south on Pacific Coast Highway, where cliffs of stone and sand loomed on the left, ocean spread below on the right, and highway curved along the coastline ahead. The sunlight piercing the haze and windshield warmed his hands, and the chill whistling past the gap in the window tousled his hair and smelled of seashore.

*That kid had better be on time*, he thought.

---

The previous night his phone awoke him.

"*Heelllloo*," he answered, dragging the word out as he held the phone to his ear.

"Dad, it's me," said the caller.

"Is everything okay?" he asked, trying to remember what night it was.

"Everything is fine," said the son. "But about tomorrow..."

"What about tomorrow?" asked the dad, a bit groggy but realizing it was Friday evening and he had gone to bed around ten to prepare for an early start in the morning.

"There's a little problem," replied the son.

The dad sat up in his bed and leaned over the nightstand to look for his glasses. He found them among the books and magazines, put them on, and glanced at the clock, displaying a quarter to midnight. "What little problem?"

"I can't spend the weekend with you."

The dad took in a deep breath and let it out slowly, the air hissing past his nose. "But we planned to spend the weekend together."

"You know how it is, Dad."

The dad inhaled another deep breath and exhaled. "Yeah, I know how it is for me, and I don't like it."

"Dad, I don't like it either, but it's not my fault you're alone."

"I didn't say it's your fault or anything about my being alone," said the dad. He hung his feet over the side of the bed, slid on his slippers, and stood up. For a moment, the conversation stopped.

"Things come up, Dad."

"Things always come up."

"Here you go again."

"Here *I* go again? You *always* do this to me!"

"I don't always do this to you!"

Realizing the discussion was becoming an argument, the dad kept silent. Neither one spoke for a minute.

"I don't get to see you much," said the dad, breaking the silence. "And when I do…" He stopped talking. Tears pooled in his eyes.

"Dad, we can meet for breakfast in the morning."

"Let's just wait until another weekend," said the dad. He paced his bedroom floor, not wanting to get angry and say something he would regret.

"No. Let's meet for breakfast in the morning," insisted the son.

"I'm tired," said the dad. "And I don't want to argue."

"I promise, we won't argue."

The dad blew out another deep breath into the phone and dabbed his eyes with a tissue from the box on the nightstand. "Meet you where?" he asked, thinking that his son was likely at a friend's house and was not going to sleep at his mother's house in Malibu.

"There's that Coast House restaurant on the water in Malibu. You know it. We can meet there," replied the son.

Rubbing his temple, the dad sat on the bed. "What time?"

"How about eight?"

"Eight!" said the dad. "I don't want to get up at six thirty, for goodness sake, just for breakfast."

"Fine," said the son.

"Fine nothing. I made plans."

"Dad, listen. I have to go. I'll see you at eight."

"Don't be late. I mean it," said the dad. He heard a click, followed by beeping. He pressed the "end call" icon.

He arrived at the Coast House at 7:40 a.m. A sign on the sidewalk read NOW SERVING BREAKFAST. Pulling into the parking lot, he did not see his ex-wife's Mercedes, the one his son usually drove when he was visiting. Two cars, however, were parked away from the building, at the far end of the lot. He parked in the space closest to the entrance.

The restaurant door was propped open, and he walked right in. Most of the lights were off, but sunlight flooded the room from the many beachside windows. A young woman, noisily putting utensils into a drawer behind the counter, saw him.

"I'm sorry, we're still closed," she told him. "We open at eight."

"Do you mind if I wait?" he asked.

"Not at all," she replied in a friendly tone.

He was standing just inside the doorway, in the waiting area, so he sat down on one of the wooden benches. For about ten minutes, he perused the pictures on the wall of Malibu in the sixties. Then he thought to call his son's cell phone to find out if he was on his way or still at home, or still sleeping—or, worse, if one of those "things" had come up and he would not be able to come after all.

There was no answer, so he left a message. "It's Dad. It's almost eight, and I'm at the restaurant."

Just as he was putting his phone back into his jeans pocket, the young woman walked over to him. She was attractive— without even trying.

"Just one?" she asked.

"No. I'm expecting someone," he said. "He should be here shortly."

She smiled and picked up two menus. "This way. I have a nice table for you."

He followed her toward the opposite side of the large room to one of the tables by the long wall, where the big open windows faced the ocean.

"How's this?" she asked, placing the menus on the table.

"Fine," he answered. "Thank you."

"Would you like some coffee while you wait?"

"That would be nice," he said, taking a seat.

"Cream?" she asked.

"Black," he said, then smiled.

She returned the smile and walked away.

Alone at the table, he looked out over the ocean and inhaled the cool air and seashore smell. The fog was gone, but several clouds glided in the sky as the sunlight glinted on the water. The waves, beating and scraping the shore, drove small vibrations up through the restaurant's floor.

The waitress soon returned with his cup of coffee.

"Here you are," she said. "Yell if you need anything." She walked back to the counter where two couples were waiting to be seated.

He sipped his coffee and, with some wonder, watched the birds just outside the open window and over the beach: seagulls screeching in flight, and out past the crashing waves, terns watching and waiting for fish while hovering in midair, then contracting and diving hard into the water, where they stayed for a while and finally popped to the surface, sometimes holding a fish.

He checked his watch: 8:36 a.m. "Late as usual," he whispered to himself.

Ten minutes later, he heard "Dad!" from across the room. As his son walked up to the table, he stood to greet him. But the young man immediately sat in the chair across from him, so there was no handshake, hug, or kiss, such as when his son was young.

"I'm sorry I'm late," said the son. "What time did you get here?"

"Before eight," replied the dad. "You know how I hate being late."

"I had to put gas in Mom's car."

The dad did not want to criticize him. He knew doing so would only ruin breakfast, the morning, the day, or even longer. "Just call me the next time if you're going to be late. Okay?"

"Okay, I'll call if I'm going to be late."

"So, how is your mother?" asked the dad, trying to be polite and wanting to get the conversation about his ex-wife out of the way.

"She's okay."

"Just okay?"

"You know how it is," said the son.

The dad nodded.

"So, are you enjoying this visit?" asked the dad, trying to change the subject.

"So far I'm enjoying it."

Then the waitress came over to their table, looked down at them, and smiled. "You good-looking gentlemen know what you'd like?"

"I'll have more coffee," said the dad.

"I'll take a Coke."

"Will you be eating?" she asked.

"We'll need a few more minutes to decide," said the dad.

"No problem," she said. "Take your time."

"Thanks," said the dad.

"And I'll be right back with your drinks."

They picked up their menus and scanned them.

"So, are you going to be staying?" asked the dad.

"Dad, we've been through this. You know I can't stay."

"No, I don't know that."

"I want to," said the son, still reading his menu.

"I want you to, also. I hardly get to see you."

"You see me when I'm in town."

"When was the last time you were in town?"

There was an awkward pause.

"What can I do?" asked the son.

"You can do plenty."

Just then a cool breeze from the open window blew a napkin across the table. The dad grabbed it in the air before it reached the floor.

"You know I miss you, son."

"I miss you too."

"I miss talking with you," said the dad.

"How about we talk more often on the phone?" asked the son.

"I call you almost every day as it is," said the dad, "and you rarely call me back."

The son said nothing. They read their menus.

A minute later the dad asked, "Just take some time to think about coming back, will you?"

"Okay, I'll think about it."

The waitress returned. "One coffee, one Coke," she said, and placed them on the table. Then she put the tray on the table behind her and took out a pad and pen from her apron. "You two gentlemen decide on anything?"

"Yes, eggs and bacon for me, please," said the dad.

"Two or three eggs?" she asked.

"Two is good, sunny side up."

"Whole wheat or white?"

"Wheat. No butter. Thanks."

"And what will you have, handsome?" she said, looking at the son.

"Do you have French toast?" he asked, holding up his menu.

"Next page," she said, and put her pen on the French-toast section of his menu.

"Great! I'll have the French toast."

"Would you like bacon or sausage?"

"Extra bacon."

"Anything else, gentlemen?"

"That's all for me," said the dad.

"Me too."

"This might take a few minutes, if you don't mind," she said, and pulled the page from the pad and put the pad and pen into her pocket.

The dad looked up at her and smiled. "No problem."

She smiled back and walked to the kitchen.

"How peaceful it looks," said the dad, surveying the ocean.

"I suppose so," said the son.

The dad stood up and moved his chair to face the window—and get closer to his son. He put a hand on the young man's shoulder. "So, how have you been?"

"Fine. Just fine."

"Do you need anything?"

"I'm fine."

"Anything at all?"

"I don't need anything, Dad."

"Money?"

"It's nothing to worry about," said the son.

"But I do worry," said the dad.

"I just have to work out a few things."

"I can work them out with you," said the dad. "You can trust me."

"I know I can trust you, Dad."

"You know, you can always move back here," said the dad. "You could stay with me."

"I would stay with you, but I can't move back now," said the son, swirling the straw in his glass.

"It's no trouble. You know that."

"I know it's no trouble," said the son, who then sipped his soda. "But you know I can't."

"No, I don't know that either."

The son stood up. "I have to wash my hands."

He walked over to the waitress, who was putting away glasses behind the counter, and asked her where the restrooms were. She pointed to a doorway at the far corner of the restaurant and he followed her direction.

Sipping his coffee, the dad watched and listened to the waves hitting the shore. His son returned five minutes later.

"What a world it is," said the dad.

Then he noticed something beyond the surf, just past the cresting waves: something swimming, slipping through the water, surfacing and submerging. "Look at that," he said, pointing toward the ocean. "See it?"

"See what?" asked the son.

"Wait. Look over there," said the dad, pointing again. "There! There it is."

"What is it?" asked the son.

"It's a dolphin."

"A damned dolphin," said the son, smirking and shaking his head.

"I suppose it is," said the dad.

"What is?" asked the son.

"Nothing," said the dad, staring at the dolphin, with its dorsal fin projecting like a small sail, its curved body forming a crescent weaving slowly in and out of the water, rising and disappearing, as if stitching the waves together.

"While driving, I've seen them along the coast in Ventura and Santa Barbara," said the dad. "I've even parked beside the beach and watched them swim past and sometimes frolic together, jumping out of the water, wrestling, having fun." He stared out across the waves and sipped from his cup. "Usually they're in groups." He could not recall ever seeing one alone. "Sometimes I see smaller ones swimming with the larger adults, families I think, and they look silver in the sunlight." *Like small charms on a bracelet*, he thought.

For a minute, they quietly watched the dolphin.

"It might be lost," said the dad, breaking the silence.

"It looks fine," said the son.

"Maybe it got separated from its group," said the dad. Frowning, he leaned toward the open window. "Maybe its family was killed."

"Killed by what?" asked the son.

"By many things. Disease, killer whales, fishing nets, people who shoot them."

"That's life," said the son.

"I'm afraid it is," said the dad, looking down and slowly nodding his head.

With a tray of food over her shoulder in one hand and a stand in the other, the waitress arrived at their table. Opening the stand, she placed the tray on it. "Here we are," she said, taking the plates from the tray and arranging them on the table.

"French toast for you," she said, "and eggs for you."

"More coffee?" she asked, looking at the dad.

"Not now, thanks."

"Enjoy," she said, then lifted the tray, folded the stand, and left.

The dad and son adjusted their plates.

Then the dad remembered something. "Several years ago, a helicopter pilot flew a few friends and me to Catalina Island. In the bright morning sun, the calm ocean below looked like a jade-green desert. We were miles out over the ocean and the water looked lifeless. Then I noticed a group of dolphins swimming straight and steady toward the island. They looked like tiny silver rips in a gigantic green sheet of fabric. They appeared determined and yet so vulnerable in that enormous ocean. I remember thinking how difficult it must be for them just to survive. And that saddened me."

"Dad...are you feeling okay?"

"I feel..." said the dad, and paused. "Do you know how very sociable they are?"

"Who's sociable?"

"Dolphins."

"Dad, they're just fish."

"They're not just fish. They're mammals."

"Okay, they're just swimming mammals."

"No, they're more than that, son. Much more. They're like us."

The dad paused, took up his knife and fork, and began to cut his eggs. His son stared at him for a moment, then picked up a bacon strip and bit it. They ate and said little to each other, except to ask how the food was or pass the salt or pepper or napkins. The son ate everything on his plate, including the orange-slice garnish. The dad ate only his eggs. Then they sat back in their chairs and looked out the window.

"Dad, are you sure you're okay?"

"Yeah, I'm just thinking."

"What about?"

"That dolphin."

"What about it?"

"That I wouldn't want to be like that dolphin."

"Why not?"

"Because it's alone," said the dad, peering into his son's eyes.

"I don't mind being alone," said the son, after a moment.

"That's because you're not alone, son."

"I've been alone, Dad, and I don't mind it."

"You're still young and strong."

"People do live alone," said the son.

"Nobody should," said the dad. "Nobody should live alone."

"But people *do* live alone."

"They don't really live," said the dad. "Not really."

Again he thought about the dolphins he had seen from the helicopter. Then he looked over the water for the silver dolphin, but it was gone.

"Nobody should live alone," he said.

———— ❦ ————

After the dad paid the bill, they walked to the parking lot. As they stood face to face by the ex-wife's car, the dad spoke first.

"Must you go, son?"

"Yes."

"So soon?"

The son nodded his head.

"Will you be returning home?" asked the dad.

"Yes." He paused. "My flight leaves on Monday."

"You can't stay?"

"I can't, Dad. I'm sorry."

"Not even another week?"

"I can't."

"I understand," said the dad, lowering his face.

"But I'll visit again soon."

"Good…That's good."

"Very soon."

"I'll look forward to it."

"Well, I should be going," said the son, reaching into a pocket for his car key.

"You take care of yourself," said the dad, pulling his shoulders back and raising his chin, trying to stand tall and proud. "And thanks for visiting."

"I'll see you soon, Dad."

"You know where I'll be," said the dad, stepping up and wrapping his arms around his son, while the young man's arms remained at his sides. "I'll miss you…I always miss you," he added, holding him tight. He kissed his son's cheek and released him. "Very much."

"I know, Dad. Me too," said the son, opening the car door. "I'll call you," he added, getting into the car and closing the door. He started the engine, waived a final good-bye, and drove away—leaving the dad behind, just watching, waving, and alone.

# THE SMALL GOLD BOX

FORTY MINUTES HAD passed since Officer Hardin had parked under an oak tree just off the side of Highway 23 around 9:30 p.m. It was raining and cold while she sat alone in her cruiser thinking.

Watching the few cars that drove by, she thought about how she had arrived where she was in her life, about her so-called career. Though she was damned lucky to still have her badge, she was now working the nighttime beat often assigned to rookies, and routinely refilling her prescriptions for sleeping pills and antidepressants.

She had spent her first two years with the force on the night shift before earning a daytime beat, back when she was a single, tall brunette with the three-days-a-week-at-the-gym body, and when men said she was beautiful and sexy. Now in her sixth year, and not a sergeant or even a corporal, she was back on another nocturnal patrol—still single but twenty-five pounds heavier—and using botulinum toxins and dermal fillers to fight back the wrinkles. "Why did that accident have to happen?" she asked herself.

The captain had assigned her to this evening shift two months ago after she had returned from seventeen months of personal leave, which should have been a suspension—without pay. Everyone around her seemed to know the reason for her absence, especially officers in her department, thanks to newspapers and online news sources.

Her career had ended nineteen months before, following her freeway car chase of a drunk driver. Officers eventually caught the inebriated man, but not until after her mistake. The investigation into her accident indicated she had been traveling about ninety miles per hour during the pursuit, but she knew she had been moving upward of one hundred and ten when she lost control of her cruiser and hit another car, driven by a father, with his son in the passenger seat. The car had flown over the guardrail and landed into one of the many oak trees in the area. The father had survived but remained unconscious and ended up in the hospital with a coma from which he never awoke. His fourteen-year-old son had died on impact.

Now she was paying for her mistake, a mistake that gave her nightmares of "paying" from behind black cold bars imbedded in gray stone walls.

Through her windshield, she saw an approaching car hurtling along the highway. She could tell it was speeding by the spray spewing from the tires and by how fast its lights were moving. The beeping from her radar gun confirmed what she already knew. Its display showed seventy-eight miles per hour, not normally too fast on a sunny day, and a speed she might have ignored if she had already eaten her midnight lunch, but on such a rainy night, she wasn't letting it pass.

She jumped her cruiser out onto the highway and soon was behind the speeding car. She turned on the emergency lights but not the siren, being in no mood to hear its blaring. The other car didn't slow down. *Give the driver a chance*, she thought. *Maybe the driver hasn't seen you or is just panicking for a minute.* Another quarter-mile went by, so she flipped on the siren, which blasted—*woo—woo—woo*. *Give the driver a chance*. A hundred yards farther and still the brake lights didn't come on. Frustrated, she picked up her microphone and shouted: "Pull over!" Ten more seconds passed with no brake lights. *"Pull over! Pull over!"* roared the speaker. The car's break lights finally illuminated bright red.

She followed the car as it pulled off to the side of the highway, onto the gravel. She hated to pull vehicles over at night on isolated roads. *No more chances.* She switched on her high beams and could see their reflection off the other car's side view mirrors. *That should help prevent anyone in it from seeing I'm alone.* She ran the car's license plate number: no outstanding tickets or warrants.

She stepped out of her vehicle and put on her hat. The rain snapped and cracked on her jacket and the hat's clear plastic cover. Flashlight in her left hand, she walked to the driver's side of the car. Her right hand, like a tarantula ready to pounce, hovered above her pistol. She saw that the driver was a woman and that she was alone. Hardin waited a moment for the driver to look up at her, but the woman kept looking down, appearing to stare at her hands on her lap. Hardin tapped the window with her flashlight. The driver, skinny in a black dress, finally looked up.

"Roll down your window," Hardin said, making a circular motion with her flashlight.

After a few seconds, the window came down.

"Do you know how fast you were driving?" Hardin asked.

"I don't know," the woman said in a weak, monotone voice that dragged out her words.

"Too fast. Much too fast for a night like this," Hardin said.

"I don't care," the woman said, looking up into Hardin's eyes. The driver's eyes were red and teary, as if she had been crying.

"Have you been drinking?" Hardin asked, seeing the blank expression on the woman's face.

"No."

"Let me see your driver's license and registration, please."

"I forgot my purse."

"So you don't have your license?"

"No, I don't."

"Is this your car?"

"Yes…sort of."

"Do you have the registration?"

"I believe so," she said. "In the glove box."

"Would you mind getting it?"

The driver leaned over, opened the glove box and rummaged inside it. Hardin put her hand on her pistol—the tarantula legs twitching. A minute later, the driver slowly sat back into her seat. She was holding a small gold box tied with red ribbon. Attached to the ribbon was a little folded card. With her head down and the box held gently in her lap, the woman began to cry.

"Ma'am, are you okay?"

The woman sobbed louder, her shoulders jerking up with every inhalation. For a minute, Hardin observed her, while raindrops, making small popping sounds, bounced off the door and hit the driver.

"Ma'am, you and your car are getting wet."

The driver just sobbed.

"Are you sure you haven't had any alcohol tonight?"

Again, the driver looked up into Hardin's eyes.

"No. I've been burying my husband," she stammered.

"Excuse me?" Hardin said, a little sarcastically. She wasn't sure she had heard correctly over the snapping sounds of the rain on her jacket and plastic hat cover.

"My husband—died on—Tuesday," the woman said, her voice strained and her words halting between sobs. "We— buried him—today." She paused, catching her breath. "There are still people at my home, and I just needed to be alone." She raised the box from her lap and held it out in front of her as if it were a delicate butterfly. "This was his car. I haven't really used it since—" she murmured, then paused. "It was to be our anniversary on that coming Wednesday. This must be...I didn't know it was here. He must have hidden it, so I wouldn't find it."

"Ma'am, what is your name?"

"Goodwin," she said softly. "Sarah Goodwin."

"Ma'am, please sit here and try to take it easy. I'm going to go back to my vehicle for a minute. I'll be right back."

Hardin returned to the cruiser while Sarah, sitting in her car with the cold wind and rain coming in, slowly opened the card. *Happy Anniversary, Myla, My Love.* Then she remembered what her husband had told her. "Myla, I got you something special for our anniversary. You'll love it." When he called her "my love," it often sounded to her like "Myla," and she would sometimes jokingly ask him, "Who is Myla?" So when he wanted to be cute, he'd call her Myla, his nickname for her.

Hardin checked the license plate number again on the computer in her cruiser. The car was actually registered to a Sarah Goodwin. The address, Hardin recognized, was in the new development, with large and expensive homes, just ten miles down the road, and she knew that buyers had only begun moving into them three months ago.

After several minutes, she was back at Sarah's window. "Ma'am, your address is 14 Hall Street, one of the new homes, right?"

"Yes," Sarah said, sniffling.

"Do you feel okay to drive?"

"Yes, I think so," she answered, appearing to compose herself somewhat, sitting up straight, putting both her hands on the steering wheel.

"Well, I'm going to follow you home, to make sure you get there safely. You can show me your license when we get there. Do you understand?"

"Yes, thank you," Sarah said. "And I'm so sorry for putting you out, especially for getting you so wet. I just needed to be alone."

"I understand. I'm fine," Hardin said.

⸺⸺

Twenty minutes later, the two vehicles pulled up to Sarah's home. The house was large, and so was the front yard. Sarah parked in the long driveway, and Hardin pulled in behind her. Hardin got out of the cruiser and walked to the side of Sarah's car. She was holding the small box in her hands, crying. Hardin stood in the cold drizzle. After a minute or so, Sarah wiped her eyes with a tissue and, having regained some composure, stepped out of her car. "Thank you for waiting," she said.

No one else was standing outside of the home, but when Sarah opened her front door and stepped into the spacious foyer and adjacent living room, a rush of people immediately surrounded her. They questioned her, thanked God, and hugged and touched her tenderly.

Then Hardin walked in, and everyone froze and stared in silence.

"It's fine," Sarah said. "I just need my license. I forgot my purse."

Hardin stood silently under the light of a large chandelier.

"I'll get my purse," Sarah told Hardin.

Sarah walked to the kitchen, her heels clicking on the marble floor.

The living room erupted with questions: "Is everything okay?" "Oh, my God, what happened?" "Was there an accident?"

"Please, I need everyone to be calm," Hardin told them.

More questions crisscrossed the room.

A minute later, Sarah returned with her license and handed it to Hardin.

"Is there a room we can talk in?" Hardin asked, ignoring the license.

"My office," Sarah said, "in the back of the house."

Hardin followed Sarah along the wide hall. They passed a large family room on the left and two bedrooms on the right before reaching the office. Hardin realized the house was larger than it looked from the front yard.

"This is a gorgeous home," Hardin said.

"I just moved in two months ago. I bought it with the money I received from a lawsuit settlement. I couldn't live in our old home."

Once inside her office, Sarah placed the gold box onto her desk, turned toward Hardin, and again offered her the license. Hardin took it. Sarah's picture, name, and age—thirty-eight—were on it.

"Under the circumstances, I think we can overlook the speeding," Hardin said, handing the license back to Sarah.

"Thank you. That's very kind of you, Officer—"

"Hardin. Linda Hardin."

The name resonated deep inside Sarah's memory and activated a part of her brain she couldn't control. Louder and louder the name echoed as her blood seemed to drain into her legs. She felt dizzy. She tottered, then dropped to the floor—unconscious.

Hardin ran to her. "Mrs. Goodwin! Mrs. Goodwin!"

Two women and a man came running into the office. "What happened?" They fell to their knees beside Sarah. "Oh, my God!"

"She just fainted," Hardin said.

"What did you say to her?" one woman asked, cradling Sarah's head.

"We were just talking, and she fainted."

"We should get her into bed."

"Should we call an ambulance?"

"Someone get some water."

Sarah stirred. "What...What happened?" she stammered.

"Sarah, you fainted, dear."

"For how long?" Sarah asked.

"Oh, you dear, not long, not long at all."

"Let's get her up." The man and a woman helped Sarah to her feet and guided her to the small sofa in the corner of the room.

"Thank you. I'm fine now. Thank you," Sarah said, sitting on the sofa.

"Sarah, you should lie down."

"Yes. Yes, I will. It was only a little low blood sugar. I didn't eat earlier. Thank you." But Sarah recalled the real reason for her blackout—and it wasn't low blood sugar.

The women and the man expressed their concerns and offered Sarah advice.

"Yes, I will lie down. I should. Definitely," Sarah told them.

"Are you sure you don't want an ambulance?"

"Yes, I'm fine now. I'll rest here. Just give me a few minutes with this nice officer."

"We'll stay with you."

"Please, everyone go back to the kitchen and living room. I'm fine. Really."

The two women and the man reluctantly left Hardin and Sarah in the office.

Sarah got up from the sofa. "Will you come with me to another room, Officer Hardin?"

"Excuse me?" Hardin said, not wanting to get deeper into the mess than she already was.

"There's something I want to show you," Sarah told her.

"I have to get back to work, ma'am."

"Yes, of course you do, but it will only take a few minutes."

Hardin paused for a moment. "I guess I can spare a few more minutes...if it will help."

"Thank you," Sarah said. "And to show my appreciation, I'd like you to have what's in this box." She stepped to her desk and picked up the gold box.

Hardin's brow furrowed, her head turned slightly to the side, and her upper body pulled back. She was confused. She didn't understand the gesture, wondered why Sarah wanted to give her what had to be a significant gift. "Uh...we can't accept gifts," she said, not knowing what else to say.

Sarah, holding out the box, stared at her. "Then help me open it."

Hardin wasn't sure what to think about this, either. *Maybe she's in shock*, she thought. *Or depression is effecting her thinking. Her brain chemicals must be off.*

"Maybe someone else in the house could assist you," Hardin said.

"No!" she blurted out. "I don't want them to know."

Before Hardin could think of the consequences, she said, "Sure, then. I guess I can do that for you."

"Let's open it in my son's room," Sarah said, and walked out of the office.

"Oh, you have a son?"

"Had. I had a son."

Hardin didn't question this. *Mind your business.*

She followed Sarah down the hall, passing several more rooms. At the end of the hall, Sarah stopped in front of a closed door. From the drawer of a small table against the wall, she removed a key, used it to open the door, stepped inside the room, and flipped the light switch. Hardin entered and saw that the room contained only a bureau and pictures, dozens of framed pictures hanging along the walls and propped on the bureau. Some of the pictures were of a man, some of a boy, some of the two together. There were no pictures of Sarah.

Hardin felt a twinge in her head, a visceral reaction from her unconscious mind. Then she felt horror. She was nauseous, and acid rose in her throat. She recognized the man and boy in the pictures—*Stephen and Scott Townsend*. The names flooded her thoughts.

"Stephen was your husband," Hardin said accusingly. "Your son was Scott."

Sarah didn't answer. She didn't have to. Hardin knew the answer.

"You're Mrs. Townsend," Hardin added, stepping back from her.

Sarah's eyes widened with the realization that what she had learned only minutes ago, Hardin now also knew.

Horrible images swamped Hardin's mind: Speeding down the freeway in her cruiser nineteen months earlier. Losing control at over one hundred miles per hour. Hitting Stephen's car. Killing his son, Scott. Hospitalizing Stephen in a permanent coma. Fighting charges of manslaughter. Praying for and hearing the not-guilty verdict. Serving the sixty days of paid suspension. Visiting her psychiatrist. The tragic events came back to her quickly. Her thoughts reeled.

"So now you know," Sarah said. "I went back to my maiden name a year ago to stop people from asking me questions about the accident."

Hardin remained silent.

"It's okay though," Sarah said. "I've decided to leave, to be with my family."

Hardin didn't know what to say. Then she said the only appropriate thing she could say. "I'm sorry! I'm so very sorry!"

"Of course you are."

"The crash was an accident."

"Of course it was an accident," Sarah said. "It's all an accident, nothing but strings of accidents. All of life is an accident." She stepped over to the bureau and opened the top drawer.

Not knowing what Sarah was searching for in the drawer, Hardin was already reaching for her pistol—the tarantula moving quickly—when she saw Sarah raise a revolver.

"Put it down, Mrs. Townsend," Hardin said, her pistol now aimed at Sarah. But before Hardin could say another word, Sarah pointed her gun.

Hardin didn't fire. Sarah had placed the gun to her own head.

"Mrs. Townsend, please don't."

Sarah reached out her left hand, the one still holding the gold box, toward Hardin. "Take this," she pleaded.

"Only if you put the gun down," Hardin said gently and slowly, holding up her left hand in the *halt* position, fingers pointing up and palm facing out.

"I can't do that," Sarah said.

"Yes, you can," Hardin said, feeling her arm muscles starting to shake.

"I've decided to leave, to be with my family."

"Put the gun down. We can talk about this."

"No. It's too late now. It's time."

But Sarah didn't shoot.

Hardin's knees began to tremble. *What am I going to do? Kill the wife too? Be responsible for killing the entire family?*

"Please, Mrs. Townsend...put...the gun...down...and talk to me. Think of your friends and family. They love you."

"No, I want to be with my family."

"Mrs. Townsend, it's been a tough day for you. You just need some rest." Hardin wanted to take these last words back as soon as she had spoken them. She was so nervous that she could hardly think. *A tough day? A tough day? How about a tough nineteen months? A tough 'the rest of your miserable life' that only one 'rest' will solve?*

"Yes, I do need rest," Sarah said.

Hardin focused on Sarah's hand and the gun. *If she points it toward me, I'll have to shoot. I must shoot.*

"It's all an accident. All of this," Sarah said.

"PUT THE GUN DOWN!" Hardin yelled. She couldn't stop herself. The words just came out. She was scared. She had never shot anyone, and she definitely didn't want to shoot Sarah. Hardin had done enough damage to this woman. And the way Hardin saw it, Sarah had a right, somewhere in the cosmos, to shoot her—dead. An eye for an eye.

A moment later, the three who had helped Sarah after she had fainted and one other woman came running into the room. There was shouting and crying and using God's name in vain. Still Hardin kept her pistol pointed at Sarah.

"Put your gun down," the man said to Hardin.

"Quiet. Everyone!" Hardin demanded. "Quiet!"

Two women—panicking, crying, ranting—left the room, and the man and one woman remained in the room with Hardin and Sarah.

"Don't shoot," the man pleaded.

"Quiet," Hardin said. "Mrs. Townsend, please put down the gun."

Sarah's gun remained planted against her head.

Hardin considered the remaining man and woman. Could they persuade Sarah to put down her gun? Or would they only worsen the potentially explosive situation? Would they interfere with what Hardin might have to do, or be injured, even killed?

Hardin decided. "You two must leave. *Now*."

"Sarah, please put down the gun. Please!" the woman said, backing out of the room.

"You too," Hardin said to the man.

"No, I'll stay."

"No, you won't. Now go." But he didn't move. "*Now*, I said."

"Do as she says," Sarah told him.

"Just don't shoot," he said, "either of you."

"Please go," Sarah begged, still standing with the muzzle pressed against her temple.

The man stared at Sarah for a moment, then gradually stepped one foot behind the other and carefully backed out of the room.

*Now what?* Hardin thought. She couldn't radio for backup because she didn't want to distract her attention from Sarah or cause her to panic and shoot herself. Besides, Hardin felt sure that at least one person who had just witnessed what was happening was on the phone with the police and that help was already on its way.

"Drop the gun, Mrs. Townsend. Just open your hand and let it fall."

"I'm so tired," Sarah said. "I need to rest."

"Drop the gun and you can go lie down on your bed. I promise."

"But the accident happened."

"We're all very sorry about that, but this isn't helping matters."

"It will help me, help it be over. All of it."

"We can get help. Would you like us to help you?"

"What about the accident?"

Hardin didn't answer but strained to think. Her concern had mostly been for Sarah's safety, but now she worried about her own. She couldn't give Sarah the chance to shoot her. *Just don't point your gun in my direction.* But could she live with herself if she killed the last member of the family? Killed the *whole* family? She needed Sarah to drop her gun.

"Let go of the gun, Mrs. Townsend...*Please!*"

"I can't."

Hardin was beginning to feel drained, tired, and she too just wanted to sit and rest. She wanted the deadlock to be over, but she didn't want anyone to die in that room.

"Mrs. Townsend, I'm going to trust you're a good woman. I'm going to put my gun down. Okay? I'm going...to put...my gun...down."

Sarah just stared at Hardin, who knew she was breaking the cardinal rule of never giving up your weapon—or putting it down. But she wouldn't shoot Sarah. She couldn't shoot her. Besides, there was a good probability her bulletproof vest would save her from a bullet—if one didn't hit her in the head. She wanted to take that chance, wanted to risk something, anything, for Sarah and her family.

"Okay, I'm putting my gun down." Hardin bent over slowly, keeping her right arm outstretched, pistol in hand, and touched the floor with the tip of the barrel. But she didn't drop the pistol. Something in her don't-be-an-idiot mind was preventing this last surrendering gesture.

"Don't do that," Sarah said.

Hardin froze, still bent over and holding her pistol.

"I can't do this myself," Sarah said.

With her head pointed up and eyes on Sarah, Hardin couldn't help thinking, *This is going to turn out badly for me, one way or another.* "If I drop my gun, you can drop yours."

"No, I can't," Sarah said. "I can't do this alone. I need help."

"We're all going to help you, Sarah. That's why we're all here—to help you."

"If I could've done it alone, I would have. So you're going to help me."

Again, Hardin was at a loss for words. She knew about people who chose *death by cop.* Every officer did. But she didn't want to be an executioner. *I can't shoot her. I won't.* She wore her badge to *protect and serve.* But she didn't protect and serve Sarah's husband and son. *Did I? No, I didn't.* So she was going to serve Sarah now, protect her from herself, from an accident.

"You owe me that," Sarah added.

And Hardin knew she did. She owed Sarah a tremendous debt. But not murder. She wouldn't murder. She couldn't. So she let go of her pistol. It made a small thumping noise on the wooden floor. *Here it comes—in the head.*

No blast and bullet.

Sarah started to cry. She lowered the gun from her temple.

Hardin slowly rose, not sure what Sarah would do next, and braced herself mentally and physically to be fired on. Her heart raced, but the exhaustion she had felt merely moments ago had vanished. Her adrenaline surged again. *I should rush her*, she thought, but she didn't. *Give her a chance.*

"You owe me! You...owe...me!" Sarah sobbed.

Hardin raised her hands, palms out, in front of her shoulders. Not quite the I-give-up posture but more like the take-it-easy gesture.

"Now, you can drop your gun, Mrs. Townsend," Hardin pleaded. "You're going to be fine."

"But you owe me. You owe me..."

"And I'll help you, but you must put down your gun. *Please.*"

"Why?"

Hardin was dumbstruck. What was she going to say: *So you can get back to your normal life? So everything will be as it was? Because life is great, and it's great to be alive?*

"Do it for me," Hardin said. "Do it for me." She couldn't believe she had actually had the audacity to say this—to her, the woman whose life she had ruined. *Okay, here it comes*, she thought. *Close your eyes.*

But a bullet didn't come. Sarah didn't shoot her.

"Why?" Sarah asked, tears in her eyes. "Why me?"

There was a pause before Hardin could answer. "Like you said, it was an accident."

"Why couldn't it have been *me* in that car?" She gazed at Hardin. "Why wasn't *I* in the car with them?"

"I don't know," Hardin answered tenderly. And she didn't know. She had spent many sleepless nights thinking about why things like that happened. *It's all an accident*, she thought, while looking into Sarah's eyes, which were pleading for answers.

"I know why. Because there's no God," Sarah said, lifting her gun and pointing the muzzle at Hardin. "I'm sorry this happened to you. I know it was an accident. But you must pick up your gun…and use it."

"Mrs. Townsend, please! I beg you, put down the gun!"

"I will count to five. If you don't pick up your gun, I'll start firing."

Hardin wet her pants.

"One."

"PUT DOWN THE GUN!" Hardin screamed.

"Two."

"Put down the gun! Put down the gun!"

"Three."

"Put—down—the—damned—guuuunn!"

"Four."

Hardin stooped to grab her pistol. *Not in the head!* she thought. *Not in the head!*

The bang reverberated throughout the house and people rushed down the hall and into the room. There stood Hardin, with her arms hanging by her sides and her pistol in her right hand. Sarah was on the floor, and half her brain was on the wall behind her.

The gold box lay open on the floor, and beside the box was a platinum ring with a yellow diamond.

The screaming began.

# Transforming Karma

A s the limousine reached the base of Samsara Mountain, the passenger saw no signs for the mountain or for Karma, nothing to indicate where he was heading or what awaited him. Approaching the gate that blocked the road heading up Samsara, the chauffeur lowered his window and stopped the limousine next to the male guard standing outside the shack.

"Passenger's name?" the guard asked.

"Andrew Benton," replied the chauffeur.

The guard scanned the tablet he held. "Please wait to the right. Proceed when the gate opens."

He had no gun, did not inspect the car or even look to see who was inside it.

The chauffeur raised his window and drove to the parking lot. "We'll be heading up the mountain in a moment, Mr. Benton. Just relax back there."

They waited ten minutes, until another limousine came down the mountain and exited the gate, before the guard waved them through.

"The drop-off point is about five miles up," the chauffeur said as they began the climb. "We'll be there in no time."

Andrew nodded and began scouring the mountainside for a building, but he saw only trees and rocks amid the mist and clouds gripping the shadowy peak crouching beneath the gray sky. Rolling down the window for a better view, he shivered as the chilled air rushed in.

The limousine snaked up the blacktop road for about twelve minutes before the chauffeur turned right, into a cul-de-sac, and stopped where a dirt path divided the trees.

"Is this the place?" Andrew asked.

"It is if you're sure," the chauffeur replied, turning his head toward Andrew. "Only if you're sure."

"Is it far?"

"I've never gotten out of the car here, never set foot on this mountain. But I've been told it's not far."

"I see," Andrew said.

"Are you feeling well enough...?"

"Yes, thank you. I'll be fine."

Understanding the chauffeur's reluctance to step onto the grounds, Andrew opened the door to get out but hesitated before placing one foot onto the graveled sidewalk, pausing, and then placing his other foot down. Standing, he felt the stones crunch under the soles of his shoes and a gust of wind shove him back. He shut the door and, by his reflection in the car's window, adjusted his yellow tie and black suit jacket. Looking up with his amber eyes, he barely felt the warmth of the obscured sun, penetrating the cold and overcast sky, on his pale and slender face. Viewing himself again in the glass, he noted his eyes looked tired: gray skin about the orbits, dark bags appearing to rest on his prominent cheekbones, and all of this framed by ear-length brown hair.

He turned to begin his ordeal, and the limousine sped away, racing its engine and squealing its tires. He stood alone, bathing in the pungent, musky odor of the decaying undergrowth around him. He reached into his inside jacket pocket and removed a tall silver flask, from which he drank a sip, and then another.

Into the woods, he trod.

Tall cedars, pines, and firs surrounded him, and as he continued to walk, the trees soon blotted out much of the sunlight and all seemed grayer.

Five minutes later, after walking about a quarter-mile, he observed through the trees the dark face of a looming building, with blacked-out windows and a stout staircase leading to its entrance. A minute later, having halted between two towering pines at the edge of the tree line, he spied a man stepping into the front door of the building, which was now about a hundred yards away. Anxious, he breathed in deeply several times—feeling his chest and back press against the lining of his jacket—before deciding to go on, to not turn back.

As he stepped out from the trees, he found the grounds bleak and brown in front of the black-skinned building, and several stone paths heading from the woods to the staircase ahead. He felt winded and his feet were heavy, but he pushed himself toward the building—to his fate.

Climbing the stairs, he strained to see through the dark windows but saw nothing past the blackened glass. When he reached the landing, the doors unexpectedly hissed open. Hearing the air whish against the doorframe, he felt the negative air pressure inside the building suck in the outside air. The effect seemed to pull him in.

Upon entering the building, he was surprised he did not find, as he presumed he would, groups of people crying, hugging, and praying: family and friends saying their last good-byes to loved ones. Nor did he see anyone who was forlorn, frightened, depressed, and ready to give up. Instead, he stood in an empty four-storied lobby with five elevators centered across the room and facing the glass windows and entrance of the building. He saw nobody until the second elevator on the left opened and a thin, brown-haired man, looking stern and purposeful in a black suit, strode toward him.

"Good day, Mr. Benton. Welcome to Karma," he said. "My name is Jason. You have an appointment with Mr. Thurnbull. He is expecting you. Right this way, please."

Andrew reached out his hand and began to speak: "I—" But Jason had already turned and was marching back to the elevator. Feeling unsettled by Jason's knowing who he was, by the quick reception and the unusual one-sided greeting, Andrew halfheartedly trailed him into the elevator, which had remained open like a gaping mouth awaiting food. Its lips hissed closed.

Not saying a word, they rode to the fifth floor of ten before the elevator stopped. The doors clanged open and Jason immediately stepped out. Andrew hesitated before exiting into the wide corridor, which was dimly lit and smelled faintly of rubber. As they walked, their heels thudding on what looked to be matte steel flooring, Andrew scanned the corridor containing closed doors and one-way glass. Then, having turned left twice, they came to a corridor in which one of the doors hung open. Jason headed straight for it.

He stopped at the open door. "Please have a seat, Mr. Benton. Mr. Thurnbull will be with you shortly."

"Thank you," Andrew said, stepping into the chilly room containing only two leather armchairs on opposite sides of a glass-topped desk. Two black-tinted, floor-to-ceiling windows filtered out much of the outside light. Hearing footsteps in the corridor, Andrew turned sharply and discovered that Jason was gone. Alone in the room, he turned to face the windows again and stole over to them. Peering out, he observed a man cross the grounds in front of the building and ascend the stairs. Suddenly a dog, perhaps a German shepherd, bolted from the trees and dashed across the grounds and up the stairs, where it and the man disappeared from view.

Andrew waited, anticipating that someone else would appear from among the trees. His intuition was right, for soon he noticed a woman walk out from one of the four paths emerging from the woods. There was something strange about her. He could see this even from the fifth floor. She carried a large, familiar bulge...*She's pregnant!* He was sure of it, especially after he watched her stop for a moment along the path to rub her protruding abdomen with both hands.

"No," he murmured, leaning in with his hands pressed hard against the glass.

"Mr. Benton," a voice said.

Andrew flinched and spun around. A tall man wearing black pants, a white shirt, and a black tie had entered the room.

"Yes," Andrew said nervously.

"I startled you," the man said, shutting the office door.

"No. No. Well, yes you did, but…"

"I was with another client," the man said, stepping around the desk and pulling out the short-backed chair. "You understand."

"Yes. Yes, of course," Andrew said, walking around to the front of the desk.

The man sat down. "Please, have a seat."

Andrew moved the chair and seated himself slowly, expecting the man to lean forward and reach out his hand to shake. "Thank you."

But the man did not initiate a handshake. Instead, he placed the black leather satchel that he was carrying onto the desk. "I'm Mr. Thurnbull. I've been assigned to review your request."

"Yes, I guessed as much," Andrew said.

And while Thurnbull delved into his satchel, pulled out a pen and cell phone, and placed them onto the desk, Andrew examined him like a coroner, from his thick black hair to his manicured nails, noticing also his trimmed eyebrows, narrow nose, and strong frame. Early forties, he guessed.

"This is an ideal spot," Andrew said, wondering what else was in the satchel.

"Excuse me?"

"What I mean is that you can see from the windows who is coming and going."

Thurnbull turned his head toward the windows. "Those coming in, yes."

While Andrew watched, Thurnbull pulled a folder from the satchel and placed it next to the phone and pen.

Looking up, a different countenance appeared to come over Thurnbull, as if he had shifted his mind into gear, ready to do his job. "I assume your ride was comfortable."

"Yes, under the circumstances," Andrew said. "Comfortable...and free."

"Of course. Any taxi, limousine, or public transportation to Karma is free to our clients," Thurnbull said, now speaking with a deeper pitch and looking directly into Andrew's eyes. "Another benefit of our service, and all paid for by our fine government."

"Well, yes, I suppose it is a benefit," Andrew said.

"We can afford to do this because the savings to the public and government that Karma provides are substantial, not only in money but in pain and suffering," Thurnbull continued. "Mass murders are down thirty percent, incarcerations nearly twenty. These benefits alone make Karma a great success and a fine investment for this country."

Andrew nodded. "Yes. Absolutely."

"And *you* are helping to maintain these benefits, Mr. Benton."

Thurnbull then looked down and pressed some buttons on the desktop's edge, revealing the glass top to be a computer screen. A white silhouette of a hand appeared on it. He placed his hand over the contour, and the computer dinged and produced icons. Then he touched them and brought up two screens, one for each side of the desk. "I think we should get straight to business," he said, "finalize everything and proceed as quickly as possible."

Andrew nodded.

With his hands interlaced and resting on the desktop, Thurnbull leaned forward, his features stolid. "So, Mr. Benton, are you ready?"

Andrew thought this question was ironic, not so much from the question itself as from Thurnbull's demeanor. He could have been asking if Andrew wanted to lease or pay cash for a new car, rather than if he was ready for a *transformation*.

"Ready as I'll ever be, or should be."

Thurnbull spread his hands and sat back. "Let's review some of the forms together, shall we? It won't take long."

"Sure," Andrew said, thinking Thurnbull was in full sales-man mode.

"Very good," Thurnbull said. "But for legal reasons, we must begin with an up-to-the-moment background check, make sure no one is using this service to escape justice or pun-ishment. We can't have that, you understand."

"Yes, of course," Andrew replied. "Absolutely. I under-stand totally."

"So, if you'll just put your right hand over the scanner in front of you," Thurnbull said, pressing icons on the screen.

Andrew watched as a white contour of a hand appeared on the right side of the screen facing him.

"Just place your hand over the outline. It will only take a moment."

Andrew looked down at his right hand as he clenched it several times.

"Mr. Benton,—"

"Yes, of course," Andrew said, placing his hand onto the screen.

A few seconds later the outline turned green and a beep sounded.

"Good," Thurnbull said. "Very good."

Andrew jerked his hand back, which was shaking slightly, and gave Thurnbull a feeble smile.

Thurnbull began pressing more icons, and files began to open on both screens.

"With your authorization and assistance, Mr. Benton, we've collected and assessed your records, including medical and financial. So, what you and I will do now is review the decision Karma has made. How does that sound to you?"

"Fine. Just fine."

"Good. Very good. Shall we continue?"

Thurnbull did not wait for a reply.

"Let me see...yes...lost your job. I see it was a great job... profitable, prestigious...unemployed for several years...crisis...lost half of your investment dollars in the stock market... son sent to prison...unavoidable...brother suicide...tragic... justifiable...understandable. Many would choose your path... decide as you have."

Andrew lowered his eyes in shame and regret.

Thurnbull looked up. "Wife died of cancer. I'm sorry, Mr. Benton, truly sorry."

Andrew's head tilted forward. "My purpose," he said softly.

"I know you've left your remaining money to your son. And as an incentive, or you can call it a reward, we have authorized the repeal of the taxes he would pay, or should pay," Thurnbull said. "His money will also be placed in a personal account for him. In addition, we will double the amount."

Andrew raised his head. "That's, uh...very thoughtful and generous," he said, his voice cracking.

Thurnbull sat straight up. "I told you this wouldn't take long. I am happy to say we have approved you for immediate action. Congratulations."

"Immediate action?" Andrew said.

"Your immediate transformation, Mr. Benton. That *is* why you're here, isn't it?"

"I thought this final meeting would determine my approval."

"Yes...yes this is...the final meeting. And we have approved your transformation."

"I thought I would have more time."

"Your time is vital to us," Thurnbull said. "So we are authorizing your request immediately. No more waiting for you."

"You reviewed everything?"

"For your well-being, Mr. Benton, let me assure you that our decision did not come easily. We considered other significant attributes of yours in determining the final verdict—no significant illnesses...clean record with no arrests...college education, master's degree...middle-aged and fit...even your

having no tattoos…no suicide attempts. We review everything. We are thorough. Thoroughness is crucial. You agree.
I'm sure."

Andrew again nodded in agreement.

"As for the final contract," Thurnbull said, "all we need
now is your signature."

He then opened the file on his desk and removed a document from it, placed his pen onto the document, and slid them
across to Andrew, who fixed his eyes on them as Thurnbull
leaned back in his chair and waited. After a few moments,
Andrew raised his gaze to Thurnbull, who returned a tight
smile. Then, slowly and delicately, Andrew picked up the pen
and studied it. It felt as heavy as a sword. He held his life in his
hand.

"Is there a concern?" Thurnbull asked, inclining forward.

"No, not at all," Andrew said, dragging the document
closer and leaning over it. But as he read, he felt time slowing,
contracting, beginning to take shape.

"No need to read it, really," Thurnbull said, breaking
Andrew's trance. "You need just sign the bottom."

Continuing to read, Andrew began biting his lower lip.
"And I can change my mind at any time, right?"

"Of course. It is your choice," Thurnbull said, folding his
hands once again.

"Even if I sign away my life?"

"That's correct."

Andrew placed the pen over the signature line, shook his
head, and signed—in midair, an inch above the paper.

Thurnbull saw he had not signed. "Mr. Benton?"

"May I get a drink of water?" Andrew asked, loosening his tie and undoing the top button of his shirt. "I'm feeling a little warm."

"Allow me to call for one of our doctors," Thurnbull said, touching icons on the screen.

"No, that won't be necessary. I'll be fine."

"Nonsense, we're here to help. We have a great staff. It's really no trouble. No trouble at all."

"I'll be okay. I just need a minute or two," Andrew said, wiping sweat from his brow with his bare hand.

Thurnbull opened a desk drawer, removed a box of tissues, and offered it to Andrew. "Please."

Andrew grabbed the box. "Thank you. I'll be fine in a minute."

"Of course."

"I just need a few minutes," Andrew said, dabbing his face and forehead with a tissue.

"Mr. Benton. Have you been taking the medications our doctors prescribed?"

Andrew's face froze. "Yes," he said, lowering his gaze and shifting in his chair. And he had indeed been taking the pills— just not every day as recommended. He figured it did not matter. Having Karma approve him and invite him to Samsara was what mattered.

Suddenly vigorous knocking rattled the door. Andrew turned his head just as the door abruptly opened. A tall, gray-haired man in a white coat entered the office.

"Doctor Greyver. Thank you for coming," Thurnbull said, standing up. "Mr. Benton feels a bit ill, I'm afraid. But I'm positive you have something to help him feel better."

Andrew, noticing the glass the doctor held—filled with what looked to be water—jumped to his feet. "I'm fine, I assure you. That won't be necessary."

"Take this, Mr. Benton," the doctor said, reaching into his coat pocket and holding out a red capsule to Andrew. "This will help you."

"It's just a little dehydration," Andrew said. "That's all. I should drink something."

"I'm sure you should take this," the doctor said, again stretching out his hand with the capsule. "It will help you."

Andrew stepped back, attempting to keep both men in view. "Thank you. I appreciate your concern," he said, holding up his hand. "But I'm sure I'm fine."

The doctor looked at Thurnbull, who gave a quick snap of his chin toward the door. The doctor placed the glass onto the desk and left the room.

"Doctor Greyver is only trying to help," Thurnbull said. "But if you think you're well enough to continue, he will be nearby."

Andrew glared at the glass. "Do you think I can get something to drink? If it won't be too much trouble. I have cash and a card for any vending machine—"

"Juice? Milk?"

"Vodka. Anything to help."

"I'm sorry, we don't have alcohol here."

"Coffee maybe. No, a Coke. Yes, an unopened can of Coke."

"Yes. Yes. How rude of me. Right away," Thurnbull declared, stepping back to his chair and sitting. "Please, Mr. Benton, sit and relax. Refreshments are on the way."

Taking deep breaths, Andrew slowly lowered himself into the chair, removed several tissues from the box, and again wiped his sweaty face.

There was complete silence for several minutes before a whining sound came from the corridor. It got louder. Thurnbull quickly stood up and hurried to open the door. Andrew turned around and saw, to his surprise, a golf cart with two men in it stop right in the middle of the corridor. He jumped up and faced the door.

The passenger stepped out of the cart and into the room, and the driver, in a black uniform, drove off. Andrew was now face to face with Jason, who held a tray on which were two bottles of water and a can of Coke.

"I'm sorry to hear you're feeling ill," Jason said. "I brought you some drinks." He placed the tray onto the desk.

"Thank you, Jason," Thurnbull said. "That will be all."

Jason gave a slight nod and exited the room, shutting the door behind him.

"Relax and enjoy your refreshments," Thurnbull said, gesturing with his open hand, up and down, for Andrew to sit.

Sitting down, Andrew thought how odd it was that the soda and water had arrived so quickly. *Nobody but the two of us heard me say what I wanted. Right?*

"Thank you," Andrew said, taking a can and snapping open the tab. He drank one gulp and held the can.

"So, where were we?" Thurnbull asked. "Yes, you were about to sign."

Andrew drank another mouthful and paused before speaking.

"Before I decide...I was wondering if I could see the trans-formers," he said.

"See the transformers?" Thurnbull said.

Andrew gave a tiny nod.

"Why?" Thurnbull asked.

"Why not?"

"Well, you'll see them when the time comes," Thurnbull told him.

"I'm sure that's true, but I'd like to see them before then."

"This is an unusual request, Mr. Benton. One I do not recommend."

"Are they that frightening?"

"No. Of course not," Thurnbull said. "It's just...not procedure."

"Then it is possible," Andrew said.

Thurnbull took in a deep breath and let it out slowly. "Of course, it's possible."

"Thank you," Andrew said, smiling slightly. "When can we arrange it?"

Thurnbull glanced at his watch. "Now, Mr. Benton. You can see them now. We have nothing to hide."

"Now? I was hoping to have more time to—"

"I will escort you to them myself," said Thurnbull, touching icons and typing on the screen. "I'll call for a ride."

Andrew raked his fingers through his hair and exhaled heavily. "Would it be possible to walk?" he asked, wanting more time to think...about his decision...and his transformation.

"It's your time," Thurnbull said, rising from his desk and going around Andrew. "If you'll follow me."

Opening the door, Thurnbull stood with his open hand directing Andrew into the corridor. As Andrew rose, Thurnbull stepped out of the office and began walking in quick strides. Hastening after and catching up to Thurnbull, Andrew remained a half step behind him.

They passed a second corridor when unexpectedly a door banged open and a woman in a white dress ran out. She was crying, covering her face with one hand and cradling her bulging abdomen with the other. As she rushed by, Andrew realized she was the woman he had seen from the office window.

He stopped, and then so did Thurnbull.

"Is she okay?" Andrew asked.

"She will be," Thurnbull replied.

Andrew frowned. "What does that mean?"

Then a man, dressed like Thurnbull—black pants, white shirt, black tie—hurried out of the room from which the woman had come. He held a phone to his ear and pushed past Andrew and Thurnbull without a word.

"She's a client?" Andrew asked.

"What do you think?"

"I think she shouldn't be here. That's what I think."

"She'll be fine," Thurnbull said. "This is a proficient facility, fully equipped, one of the best."

"But will she be okay?"

Thurnbull stopped short and turned to Andrew. "I'm afraid that really is…none of my business."

Realizing Thurnbull was telling him to mind his own business, Andrew nodded. "I see."

Thurnbull resumed his brisk walk. Andrew shadowed him.

They soon passed two doors, one with a white symbol of a woman and the other of a man—restroom doors.

"I could use a minute," Andrew said.

Thurnbull again halted and pivoted round. Andrew pointed to the men's room.

Thurnbull exhaled audibly. "By all means."

Andrew pushed past the door into the restroom and entered a stall. He listened for Thurnbull. No Thurnbull. So he took out his flask and downed a slug. "Thank God," he said to himself, and rushed to wash his hands and exit back into the corridor.

"All set," he said, seeing Thurnbull eyeing his watch.

Thurnbull said nothing but turned and renewed his hurried gait.

Along the next corridor, they came to a sitting room with two small sofas. The chamber was dismal, its gloom pierced by a single shaft of light from the ceiling. Beneath the confined beam, a portly, bald man of about sixty, in a black suit, stood grimacing with tightly closed eyes and taut lips. Andrew could see the deep concentration, or perhaps pain, in the man's face.

"Hold up," Andrew said to Thurnbull.

As Andrew approached the man, the man's lips mumbled and his clenched hands trembled. A crucifix dangled from a chain around his neck. Then Andrew spotted the white rectangle centered over the man's throat.

Andrew started back a step. "Excuse me, Father!"

The man's eyes opened and his eyebrows rose, looking surprised to see Andrew.

"You're a priest," Andrew said.

"What's that?" the man asked.

"Priest. You're a priest."

Tilting his head back and squeezing his eyes shut, the man began massaging his forehead with his index and middle fingers.

"I'm a priest," he stammered, as if he was not sure, or was trying to convince himself.

"Are you okay, Father?" Andrew asked. "You look troubled."

Opening his eyes, the man scanned Andrew's face. "Who is not troubled in this place?"

"Father, I didn't expect to see you here. The happenings and all."

"Here?" the man said. "I know no other place more in need of me."

"Father!" Thurnbull exclaimed. "You know the rules."

The priest's lips tightened and his eyes narrowed, but he did not look at Thurnbull.

"Yes, I know the rules," the priest said. "And I know what I should do."

Thurnbull's posture stiffened. "Please excuse us, Father," he said. "Mr. Benton and I are in a hurry."

Andrew glowered at Thurnbull. "Just a minute. One minute."

"I'm sorry, Father," Andrew said, turning back to the priest.

"You don't work here, do you?" the priest asked, touching Andrew's arm.

"No, Father, I don't," Andrew said. "I'm—"

"A visitor," the priest interrupted.

"Yes, Father...a visitor."

"Are you confirmed yet?"

"What do you mean?"

"Confirmed," the priest repeated, searching Andrew's eyes. "Have you made your final decision, signed the contract?"

"No...not yet," Andrew said. "I don't believe so."

"Father," Thurnbull interrupted. "You know you can't ask those questions."

"When they concern life and death," the priest told him, "I ask the questions."

Thurnbull glared at the priest but spoke to Andrew. "We must get going, Mr. Benton."

"We don't have much time," the priest said, grabbing Andrew's hand.

"Mr. Benton," Thurnbull said. "Please."

"Yes, I'm coming," said Andrew. But he did not move.

The priest bowed his head and muttered something Andrew could not make out. Then he took his crucifix and touched it to Andrew's forehead. "Go in peace, my son."

"But I'm tired."

"Yes."

"Sick and tired."

"Yes, I know."

"You'll pray for me, Father?"

"I'll pray for both of us, but you must go, my son. Have faith."

"Father, please," Thurnbull said.

The priest's eyes locked on Thurnbull, who just shook his head. The two men appeared to understand each other. Then the priest turned back to Andrew.

"Go now," the priest told Andrew.

Andrew slowly pulled back his hand, which the priest had held.

"Good-bye, Father."

"God be with you, my son."

Thurnbull turned to walk away. "Mr. Benton."

As Andrew turned, Thurnbull started walking up the corridor. Andrew followed him.

At the end of the corridor, they came to a long descending escalator.

Thurnbull stopped and faced Andrew. "Please wait here, Mr. Benton," he said. "I forgot to provide Father Balsa with some information. I won't be long."

Andrew watched Thurnbull walk back to the priest. They began talking, and after a minute, the priest reached into his jacket pocket and pulled out a small black book that he pumped up and down in front of Thurnbull while they argued. Several more minutes passed before Thurnbull left the priest and returned to Andrew.

"Thank you for waiting," Thurnbull said.

"Is everything okay?" Andrew asked.

"Yes, of course. Father Balsa and I were discussing his next assignment."

"Discussing? His assignment?"

"Yes. He works here."

Thurnbull stretched his open hand toward the escalator. "We're going down."

Andrew stepped onto a metal stair, with Thurnbull behind him. They descended three floors to the bottom of the escalator, where they stepped off and onto a wide railed terrace on the second floor.

They now stood in the back of the building, overlooking several acres of groomed lawn and landscaped gardens comprised of small trees, shrubs, and bushes. On their right, adjacent to the building, there loomed an enormous rock face topped with tall conifers. And at the base of this cliff, three massive white holes were built side by side into the stone. They were bright and smooth, and large enough to drive a bus into. Nothing gave away what awaited inside or beyond them.

The whole scene was clean, serene, and welcoming, yet at the same time fearsome. Everything appeared as one might imagine it should.

"That must be them," Andrew said, pointing to the three white tunnels.

"Watch," Thurnbull said, pointing to the opposite end of the grounds.

"Watch what?" Andrew asked.

Thurnbull did not answer. He did not have too, for across the lawn in front of them, about a hundred yards away, a man arose from a row of sheltered escalators coming up out of the ground and ascending to the lawn. He proceeded to walk casually along one of the straight dirt pathways, which traversed the lawn and passed the gardens, before he turned left into one of the white openings, the first of the three he came to.

Dismayed at witnessing the man execute the deed so calmly, Andrew placed his right hand over his left chest—feeling the flask through his jacket.

Then another man rose into view from another of the escalators, and he too progressed down one of the paths and into the third cavity, the one farthest away from the escalators and closest to the building—seeming to delay his fate a little longer by passing the first and second transformers, before finally entering the third.

"They seem peaceful, accepting. They just walk up and in," Andrew said.

"Of course. Why shouldn't they be?" Thurnbull said.

"They're going to their end," Andrew said.

"We don't know that. It might be a new beginning for them," Thurnbull said.

"You believe that?" Andrew asked.

"I must."

"But do you believe it?"

"It is their choice," Thurnbull said, sidestepping the question. "And for all of them it's the right choice. We make sure of it. They're sure of it."

"What if they're not sure of it?"

"Then they can always change their minds."

"Change their minds?"

"Why, yes. It happens, though not often, but it happens. And when it does...procedures are followed."

Andrew thought about this for a minute. Thurnbull was silent but glanced at his watch.

"Up to what point can a person change his mind?" Andrew finally asked.

"Up until the very point at which his mind makes the change."

Andrew paused for a moment, taking time to think. "You mean right before entering the transformers."

"Some have stepped in and then out, changing their minds at the very last second."

"There must be a scene."

"No scene. We have *friends* to assist them...guide them to another area for what could be called a...debriefing."

"What if they change their minds again and want to...go through with it?"

"If the debriefing is not completed, they can be guided back to the gardens to proceed again with their journey. If the debriefing process has concluded, they can always reapply. There's no certainty they'll be accepted again, but their circumstances would be reassessed."

"How many change their minds?" Andrew asked.

"I really cannot discuss that. We don't wish that information to prejudice or discourage people from looking into our services. You understand."

"I guess so." Andrew said.

Then, changing the subject somewhat, Andrew asked, "Will it be painful? Will I know what's happening to me?"

"No more than the knowing and pain you felt on the hand scanner in my office," Thurnbull said. "Besides, our doctors provide wonderful medications for people facing *transformation*."

Andrew nodded his head in understanding.

"It's all done in the most humane and comfortable way possible. Don't you agree?" Thurnbull said.

Again, Andrew nodded in agreement.

Then he noticed another figure leaving the escalator area and walking toward the three large openings in the side of the mountain. She soon disappeared into the central opening. Andrew heard no sound and saw no flash, nothing at all to indicate a transformation had just taken place. Then he stumbled back from the rail as an overwhelming feeling came over him—loneliness. From what he had witnessed, he now realized that transformation was a personal event, one of solitude, faced and experienced only by the person being transformed.

"As you see, the process is quick and easy," Thurnbull said. "You agree?"

Andrew just looked at him.

"Well then, should we proceed back to my office?"

Then from an escalator rose a man, the one Andrew had seen from the window in Thurnbull's office, the one in the gray suit, and he was holding the shepherd dog, carrying it against his breast. He walked to the center of the lawn and placed the dog down, where he proceeded to hug and kiss his four-legged friend. Andrew's face crumpled with sadness, and tears swelled in his eyes as he realized that the dog had devotedly pursued its master to and into the building—as if it knew where its master was going, knew he would not return.

Now, from below Andrew's view, seeming to come from the building, a man in a black uniform walked out to the man and dog. The two men looked to be speaking when the man in the gray suit handed his dog by the leash to the man in black. The man in gray then knelt down and, with his hands cradling the dog's face, once again kissed his friend. Then while the uniformed man held the dog back, the gray-suited man walked away and toward the central portal. The dog rose onto its hind legs, pulling and barking. And as the suited man approached the opening, he turned and waved to his distressed friend. But just as the man turned back toward the opening, his dog went crazy, turning its head and biting the hand holding its leash. Now free, the dog dashed toward its master, but it was too late. The man was gone, and soon so was the dog, for it followed its master into the void. Tears poured from Andrew's eyes and rippled down his cheeks.

And as more tears rose in his eyes, two more men rose from the escalators across the lawn. They passed through the openings before he caught sight of the white dress. The pregnant woman was walking on a path, toward the transformers. Then a man in a black suit came running up from an escalator opening and out onto the lawn and up to the woman in white.

"That's Father Balsa!" Andrew cried.

Father Balsa and the woman appeared to be talking when he took her hand and began walking her toward the central opening. They were five feet from the entrance when their hands released, but Father Balsa did not stop. He walked with the woman, side by side, step by step, until...they disappeared.

"He wasn't authorized!" Thurnbull exclaimed.

"He wasn't authorized?" Andrew said. "He wasn't authorized? That's what you have to say?"

"Mr. Benton, excuse me, but we have rules."

Andrew wiped his jacket sleeve across his face, removing tears. "I'm sure Father Balsa had rules too."

"You're upset," Thurnbull said. "We should get back to my office."

"I'm upset! *I'm* upset! Sure, I'm upset. Who wouldn't be?"

"Please control yourself," Thurnbull said.

The man on the lawn in the black uniform looked up toward the terrace and started walking toward the building.

"I think I'm going to be sick," Andrew said.

"We'll get you something from the doctor on our way back to the office."

"Yeah, something strong—whiskey," Andrew said.

"I'm sorry, we don't have alcohol at this facility."

"Well, you should. Lots of it."

"We should go," Thurnbull said.

"Good idea," Andrew said. "I want to go home."

"Home!" Thurnbull exclaimed.

"Yes, home. I want to go home. I've seen enough."

"As I said, Mr. Benton, we have rules, and I have a job to do."

"Yes," said Andrew, "and I'll bet Father Balsa had a job to do too."

Thurnbull stood up straight, puffing out his chest.

"Your job is to convince persons to go one way," Andrew said, "and Father Balsa's job was to convince them to go another, I suppose. But for some reason, I don't know why, you won.

I assume many more people walk through those transformers than walk out the front doors of this building."

"Mr. Benton, this facility is necessary and a profitable addition to society."

"Yes it is. Maybe. But at what cost? What are we giving up? I don't know right now, and I don't have the time to contemplate it, but it might be our humanity that we're giving up. Are we trading our humanity for convenience, for some safety, some profit? Is it worth it? Will it be worth it in the future? Where are we headed? Tell me that!"

"We can discuss this in my office."

"I'm not sure what I witnessed down there from Father Balsa and that dog. Was it love? Was it compassion? I just don't know, but I want to."

"It's over now," Thurnbull said.

"Loyalty!" Andrew interjected. "I witnessed loyalty...from both of them. They showed loyalty. They were loyal...to the end."

"Calm yourself, Mr. Benton."

"Will you stop doing that, stop using my name? It makes me feel like you're trying to sell me...like you feel you're better than me...know more than I do."

Thurnbull did not defend himself. He was looking down the corridor to their left. Then Andrew noticed three men in black approaching from that direction. The man in front was wearing a uniform, but the two men behind him looked to be clad in some sort of padded gear and helmets. The three men marched right up to them.

"Is there a problem?" the man in the black uniform asked. "I heard yelling."

Thurnbull looked at Andrew. "No. No problem. We were just heading to my office."

"Should we accompany you?" the man asked Thurnbull.

"No. I don't believe that'll be necessary," Thurnbull told him. "You may go."

The three men turned around and left, but not before the black-uniformed man gave Andrew a momentary glower.

"What was that all about?" Andrew asked Thurnbull.

"Precaution," Thurnbull said, and began walking.

Andrew followed him.

---

With both men again seated in the office, Thurnbull directly resumed the process.

"As defined in your paperwork, this meeting could authorize immediate approval, and you are now approved. Are you ready to sign?"

*No, I'm not ready! Are you crazy?* thought Andrew. "I'd like some time to think it over."

"That's fine," Thurnbull said. "We have lovely waiting areas and contemplation rooms available——"

"At home, Mr. Thurnbull. I would like to go home…and think about things."

"I see…yes…this sometimes happens…not often, of course, but it does happen. Most people are certain about their decision before they come to this final meeting. But as I said, this sometimes happens."

"Well, I'm glad your company has made provisions for this sort of thing," Andrew said, rising from his chair. "And I wouldn't want you to think I'm rude, but I am getting a little hungry, so I'm going to leave now and go home and make my decision. You'll hear from me soon. Very soon."

Thurnbull rose from his seat. "It's entirely your choice, Mr. Benton."

"I'll call you...very soon," Andrew said, while backing up to the office door. "You'll hear from me."

"Please, let me get Jason to escort you."

"No, that's not necessary," Andrew said. "I can easily find my way back down."

He opened the door and stepped into the corridor. He did not look back at Thurnbull or shut the door behind him. Seeing nobody else about, he promptly strode to the elevators and pressed the call button. Moments later, the elevator doors opened. He rushed inside, and the doors sealed shut. Down it went. He counted to himself, *four...three...two... one...*

The elevator stopped, but the doors did not open. He waited anxiously, sweat starting to form on his forehead. After almost a minute, he hit the doors with his palm. Nothing. Several minutes passed, and just as he was beginning to feel claustrophobic, the doors sprang apart. He lurched back to the rear wall of the elevator; facing him were four masked men wearing what looked like black body armor. They rushed him and gripped his arms and wrists.

"What?...What is this?...Hey!...Let me go!" The doors hissed shut. He felt heavier as the elevator launched upwards.

He threatened and cursed the men as they dragged him back to Thurnbull's office.

"What the hell is this?" Andrew demanded of Thurnbull.

"Precaution."

"You call this precaution?" Andrew fumed, spit flying from his lips. "Let me go!" he shouted, twisting left and right as the men tightened their grips.

"Let him go," Thurnbull ordered.

"Precaution, my ass," Andrew said, dropping his arms heavily to his sides.

"We have rules, Mr. Benton. I've told you that."

"Yeah, well, you need to be a little more specific."

"You may go, gentlemen," Thurnbull said.

"Gentlemen, my ass," said Andrew, brushing the wrinkles out of his jacket with his hands.

The men departed—slowly—adjusting their body armor as they did so.

Thurnbull pulled out his chair. "Have a seat, Mr. Benton. Please."

"I don't want a seat. I think I made that clear."

"Mr. Benton, I'm just doing my job."

"What job is that?"

"Let's just follow the procedures and all will be fine."

"All will not be fine. *I'm* not fine. It's not *fine*."

"Well, let's just continue with the procedures, so you can be on your way."

"Good," Andrew said.

"And remember, Mr. Benton, you came to us."

Andrew took several long, deep breaths and then sat down.

"Thank you," Thurnbull said, also taking a seat.

Andrew was quiet. He retrieved his flask, untwisted the cap, and took a quick hit.

Thurnbull's eyes followed it.

"Precaution," Andrew said, sarcastically.

"Shall we proceed?" Thurnbull asked, returning the sarcasm.

Andrew sighed. "I just want to get this over with."

"Okay then," Thurnbull said. "It stipulates here in the contract that—"

A sharp, cracking sound infiltrated the room, and the window now had in its glass a small round web with a sunny hole in its center. Andrew jerked up, gripping the chair's armrests, and thought he saw a large red flag fall through the air, just beyond the windows.

*Crack!*

A second hole with lighted tendrils spread in the glass. Andrew dove behind the desk. Thurnbull's knees banged the inside of the desk as his chair screeched against the floor. A heartbeat later, he too plunged to the floor, where he cowered beside Andrew.

"Someone's shooting!" Andrew said.

Thurnbull was silent. Andrew could feel Thurnbull's trembling hand on his back.

Listening as hard as he could, Andrew could hear nothing but his own heavy breathing—and Thurnbull's. They stayed still and waited for what felt like five minutes. Then Andrew heard footsteps running in the corridor and "Is anyone hurt up here?"

Thurnbull scurried to the door on his hands and knees, opened it, and peered around the jamb. "Over here! Over here!" he yelled.

"Stay down! Don't move!" the voice from the corridor said.

A crouching man in a black uniform appeared by the door. "Are you okay?" he asked.

"I think so," Thurnbull said. "Two shots came through the window."

"Are you hurt?" the man asked Thurnbull.

"No. I don't think so," Thurnbull said. "But what was that?"

"We received a phone threat earlier, supposedly from a man whose girlfriend was on her way here," the man said. "We believe he's on the grounds, that he parachuted in."

*Parachute?* Andrew thought. *Not a flag.*

"Does this happen often?" Andrew asked, coming out from behind the chair.

"I'm sorry, sir," the man said to Thurnbull. "I thought you were alone."

"It's okay," Thurnbull told him. "He's a client. He's being processed today."

Not liking the comment and feeling insignificant, Andrew opened his mouth to speak but checked himself, pursing his lips and flaring his nostrils and exhaling audibly through his nose.

The man straightened up. "All right then. You two just stay put. Don't move until we find out what's going on."

He rushed back up the corridor, talking to his lapel, into what Andrew assumed was a microphone, and disappeared into a side corridor.

"So do they?" Andrew asked.

"What's that?" Thurnbull asked.

"Do things like this happen often?"

"No. They *don't*," Thurnbull said, with a firm assurance Andrew did not trust.

"Obviously not everyone believes Karma is a good thing," Andrew said.

"Yes, but you do," Thurnbull said.

"I did," Andrew said. "I don't know now."

Thurnbull then scampered on all fours into the office, grabbed his cell phone off his desk, and scooted back to the doorway, where he rose to his feet and began running up the corridor. "Stay here," he called back to Andrew.

"What!" Andrew exclaimed. "You're not going to leave me here alone, are you?"

Thurnbull stopped and turned. "It's better for you to stay put."

"Better?" Andrew exclaimed. "You mean safer, don't you?"

"No!" Thurnbull said. "You're safe here, but I can't have you walking about until we're sure——"

"Sure that I'll be *safe*?"

"Just wait here!" Thurnbull shouted. "I don't have time to debate this. Just *stay* here!"

"Leave me a gun at least!" Andrew cried.

Thurnbull paused a moment before shouting back. "No guns!"

"What do you mean, no guns?"

"There are no guns here!"

"What! How about security?"

"Just stay there!"

"All right!" Andrew shouted.

Thurnbull dashed to the elevators and pressed the call button. He glanced back at Andrew, who still stood in the doorway. Seconds later, the bell dinged and the doors opened. But Thurnbull did not step forward. Instead, he stumbled backwards as a pistol emerged, chest high, from the elevator. The man gripping the pistol shoved him against the wall. Before Andrew could get out of sight, the man looked down the corridor and spotted him.

"You!" the man yelled. *"Don't move!"*

The man, who wore olive-green clothing, said something to Thurnbull and prodded him with the pistol to walk toward Andrew.

As they approached, Andrew raised his hands above his head. The man looked him up and down.

"Who in hell are you?" the man asked Andrew.

"He's a client," Thurnbull said.

"I didn't ask you," the man said. "You just shut up."

The man glared at Andrew. "I asked you a damn question."

"I had an appointment today," Andrew stammered.

"You don't work here?" the man asked him.

Andrew shook his head.

"And what about you, bigmouth?" the man asked, jabbing the pistol into Thurnbull's chest. "Do you work here?"

Thurnbull glanced at Andrew.

"Don't look at him," the man said, poking him harder. "*I'm* talking to you."

"Yes," Thurnbull said.

"Yes, what?"

"I work here," Thurnbull said.

"Okay, now we're getting somewhere," the man said. "And you...drop your damn hands."

Andrew lowered them slowly to his sides.

"I'm here to get Maria Gale," the man said to Thurnbull. "Where is she?"

Thurnbull did not respond.

"Where—can—I—find—her?" He emphasized each word.

"I don't know," Thurnbull said.

"What are you saying, you don't know?" the man asked, taking a step toward Thurnbull.

"She's not one of my clients," Thurnbull answered.

"There must be a list, or waiting area, something," the man said. "I have to find her!"

"Counselors deal only with clients assigned to them," Thurnbull said. "She's not one of mine."

"How do I find out who is her...What did you call them? Counselors?"

"We don't have access to names assigned to other counselors," Thurnbull replied.

"There must be a sign-in sheet or a security list."

"No sheets. No lists," Thurnbull said.

"Do *not* test me!"

"Each counselor learns specifics about their clients," explained Thurnbull. "We know exactly when they arrive, know what they look like, and promptly greet them when they get here."

"You can call someone then, a manager, the head of counselors," the man said.

"We, and any assistants or personnel working here, don't discuss clients or have access to files that don't pertain to our own clients."

"Clients! Clients! You call them clients," the man cried. "They're victims. That's what they are. *Victims!*"

Thurnbull lowered his head.

"You must have access to lists of *clients*," the man said threateningly.

"I don't even have a list of my own clients," Thurnbull said. "Once clients have been processed, their files disappear from our computers."

"Processed!" the man said, again getting in Thurnbull's face. "You mean killed. *Murdered!*"

The man bit his bottom lip and his face contorted into grotesque shapes.

"How can I find her? *How!*" he screamed into Thurnbull's face.

Thurnbull jerked back, and his hands and arms began to tremble. "We can…look around…for her," he stammered.

"She's blond, possibly in a white dress," the man said. "The voicemail she left me said she was wearing her wedding dress."

Andrew gasped and slowly turned his gaze to Thurnbull, who focused on Andrew and then the man, and back to Andrew.

"What's going on?" the man asked. "Have you seen her? *Have you!*" He waved his pistol back and forth at Thurnbull and Andrew.

Thurnbull shook his head. Andrew lowered his eyes.

Awkward silence hung in the air.

Andrew finally lifted his head and looked at the man. "Was she...pregnant?" he asked reluctantly.

Thurnbull whipped his head toward Andrew with a look of disbelief, his eyes bulging and his mouth agape.

Andrew's lips trembled.

The man lowered his pistol. "You've seen her," he said to Andrew.

Andrew waited a moment before nodding.

"Where? When?" the man asked.

Feeling pangs of remorse and guilt and anger all at once, Andrew looked at Thurnbull and blurted out, "*He* can tell you."

The man turned on Thurnbull again. "Where is she?" he demanded, pointing the pistol directly at Thurnbull's forehead.

"I...I..." Thurnbull stammered.

"Where?" the man shouted, dropping the butt of the pistol down onto Thurnbull's shoulder—hard.

"Ahh!" Thurnbull moaned, dropping to one knee and grimacing in pain. But he did not answer.

"I'll give you five seconds to tell me where she is," the man said, aiming the barrel at Thurnbull's temple, "or I'll blow your murdering head off."

Thurnbull began to hyperventilate but said nothing.

"One...Two...Three..."

"Tell him!" Andrew cried.

Still grimacing, Thurnbull shook his head and exhaled sharp, audible breaths.

"We saw her near the transformers," Andrew said breathlessly.

"What are you saying? When!"

Andrew took in a deep breath and let it out slowly. "I'm not sure if it was her, but the woman wore a white dress...and she looked pregnant."

"She *is* pregnant. We were going to get married, but we called the wedding off. I called it off."

The man turned away from Thurnbull and Andrew. Thurnbull struggled to his feet.

"Her dress is missing. It's knee length and strapless."

The man was pacing from wall to wall.

Andrew thought back and realized the dress the woman had worn matched that description. *It must have been her.*

"So she's gone?" the man asked, stopping and turning to Andrew.

Andrew looked at Thurnbull, who nodded his head.

"Yes," Andrew said.

The man turned and fired a bullet that ripped through Thurnbull's arm.

*"Ahh! Aaahh!"* Thurnbull shrieked, then shrieked some more—and louder still.

The man aimed at Thurnbull's chest.

"No!" Andrew yelled. "Don't kill him...Please!" he added, stepping in front of Thurnbull, who was still screaming in agony.

"Why not!" the man shouted. "They killed my Maria!"

"It's not his fault!" Andrew cried.

"Not his fault! Not his fault!" the man shouted. "She'd be alive if not for this company and people like *him*." He pointed the gun at Thurnbull.

Andrew let out a deep breath. "You might be right, but I'm here, and he didn't force me to come. I asked to come."

"What does that have to do with anything!" the man cried.

"Everything!" Andrew exclaimed. "But who is to blame is not the issue right now. You can't kill this man. Please, I beg you. Don't kill him."

Thurnbull was still writhing in pain, moaning and rocking and clutching his arm, while the man stood frozen with his pistol drawn, this time at Andrew, who was fighting to remain standing, despite the onset of dizziness and blurred vision. Seconds passed.

The man did not fire, but again started in on Thurnbull. "Tell him," he demanded, poking the pistol into Thurnbull's head. "Tell him the big secret, the one you don't want the public or anyone interested in your service to know. Tell him how many people leave this place after coming here. Tell him!"

Thurnbull, clenching his teeth so hard that his jaw muscles flexed, glared at the man.

"*I said tell him!*" the man shouted.

Fighting the pain, Thurnbull managed to say, "None."

"What was that?" the man asked.

Thurnbull coughed several times. The man glowered at him, waiting.

"No one...leaves," Thurnbull stammered.

Andrew drew in a sharp breath and his head jerked back. "No one leaves?"

"Not the way they came in," the man said.

"You mean——" Andrew gasped.

"That's exactly what he means," the man said. "Everyone who enters this hellhole is processed. *Everyone.*"

The man punched Thurnbull square in the solar plexus. Thurnbull dropped hard, gasping for breath. The man smiled and nodded his head.

"Enough!" said Andrew, throwing his arm up in front of the man.

Thurnbull managed a deep inhale and stared up pitifully at Andrew.

"He's had enough," Andrew said.

"Really?" the man said. "He hasn't told you all of it."

Andrew whipped his head around to Thurnbull.

"Tell him," the man ordered. "Tell him about you and all the others who work and live here. Tell him why you live underground and never leave the mountain. Tell him."

Thurnbull closed his eyes and began to sob.

The man kicked him. "Now, now. None of that."

Andrew pushed himself in front of the man. "Let him be!"

"Let him be! Let him be!" the man cried, jerking the pistol up to Andrew's face. "Why couldn't he just let *others* be?"

"I don't know," Andrew said. "But he's had enough."

Thurnbull's chest was heaving and his arms, hands, lips, and legs were trembling.

The man turned his pistol from Andrew to Thurnbull.

"Kill me!" Andrew shouted. "Kill *me* if you have to kill! That's why I'm here. Kill me!" he added, spraying spittle into the man's face.

The man lowered his pistol and shook his head for several seconds. "Give me one good reason not to kill this *scum*."

Andrew knew the answer immediately. The reason had been tormenting him for years, torturing him with regret. "Purpose," he exclaimed. "I need purpose."

The man took several deep breaths, then tapped the muzzle of his pistol against Andrew's arm. "Let me get this straight. You want to save this man?"

"I need to," Andrew said.

"Need to? You need to?" the man echoed.

"Yes," Andrew whispered.

The man waited a minute, biting his lower lip.

"Okay...Okay...On one condition," he said.

"What?" Andrew asked.

"You live, and I get to see the transformers."

"What?"

"If you live, then he lives," the man said.

Andrew looked down at Thurnbull.

"All right," Andrew said. "I won't go through with my transformation."

"And the transformers?" the man asked. "I need to get to them...fast."

Andrew again looked down at Thurnbull, who was still shaking on the floor and appeared to be in shock.

"I'll show you," Andrew said. "They're in the back of the building."

Andrew slowly knelt next to Thurnbull. "Stay here," he whispered. "I'll notify the first person I see. I'm sorry."

Andrew rose to his feet. "Let's go," he said to the man.

Andrew rushed down the corridor, retracing his earlier path. The man hurried behind him. They reached the escalator and went down. At the bottom, two men in black uniforms approached them.

"Stop!" Andrew called out, holding up a hand. "He has a gun. Mr. Thurnbull has been shot and is bleeding in the corridor. Fifth floor I think. Hurry. Go! Go!"

The two men looked at the man and the pistol.

"Go. I'll be okay," Andrew told them. "There'll be no more shooting," he added, looking into the eyes of the pistol-wielding man.

The men dashed off. Andrew watched them leave.

"They'll call security," Andrew said. "They'll stop us."

The man smirked. "There is no security here."

"What do you mean?"

"Not the kind you think. No weapons are allowed here."

"What?"

"Government regulations. No one can have weapons here."

"No one?" Andrew asked.

The man shook his head.

Andrew paused for a moment. "I see."

Then slowly he walked over to the railing. "There they are," he said, pointing to the gaping mouths in the rock face.

Gripping the railing, the man looked out at the transformers, then up at the sky, and back at the transformers. "So this is what we've come to."

Andrew nodded.

"God pity us," the man said, shaking his head.

Again, Andrew just nodded.

For a minute, neither man spoke.

"You know," Andrew said, breaking the heavy silence. "He never said why the people who work here never leave this mountain."

The man looked deeply and warmly into Andrew's eyes. "They're processed. All of them are processed."

Andrew stood motionless. *They're just like everyone else*, he thought. *That's why they work so hard to process people. They have to believe it's just, beneficial to humanity, morally acceptable, painless.*

"They can't leave?" Andrew asked.

"Oh, they can leave…the same way you can," the man said, pointing his outstretched arm like an arrow, his finger aimed at the transformers. "There. There are the exits."

Andrew looked at the transformers, wishing they would just disappear.

"So what now?" he asked.

"Life goes on," the man said.

"What do you mean?" Andrew asked.

"We make a trade."

"I don't understand."

"My life for yours."

"What do you mean?"

"You agreed to live...I did not," the man said, handing the pistol to Andrew, who took it slowly and then let it drop to his side.

"You can go. You're free to go," the man said.

"But...But—"

"I can't live without her," the man said. "I can't."

Andrew paused and thought about why he had come to Karma, the main reason, the unbearable reason. "I understand."

The man gave a faint smile and stared into Andrew's eyes.

"This is good-bye," the man said, reaching out his hand.

Andrew took his hand and shook it gently. "Good-bye... and thank you."

Then the man unzipped his jacket and revealed a vest covered in wires and rectangular shapes. "Go now."

Andrew backed up slowly, carefully, keeping his eyes on the man.

"Go!" the man said.

Andrew ran.

The explosion at the transformers' entrances was deafening, destructive, awesome, redemptive, hopeful.

Nine months later, Jason exited an elevator to greet a client in the massive lobby of the Karma building.

"Good day, Mrs. Taylor. Welcome to Karma," he said. "My name is Jason. You have an appointment with Mr. Benton. He is expecting you."

# Reflections of
# a Blue Moon

In my thoughts she dwelled
Recalled love was hell
Vengeful deed to tell

WHY AM I writing this story? Guilt? No, not guilt. To hell with guilt. Redemption? Yes, redemption. Now, I know I cannot hope for it in this life, but I can pray to receive it for my soul in the next life—after death—by preventing another from suffering the fate to which I have condemned myself. Therefore, I beseech you who read my testimony to avoid what I have done, and be careful about what you pray for.

You might after reading this think I'm mad, so let me assure you I'm not. This isn't a story. It really happened. And being the only person who knows what truly occurred that night, I swear to God I will reveal everything for the first time. I have nothing to gain by lying.

Now, before I begin my story, I need to say I accept full responsibility for executing the incident but not for what eventually transpired—I'm innocent of that.

Here is how I remember the accursed event. I was driving north on the wide, reflector-lined freeway, heading into the mountains, with my truck's headlights clearing a passage through the darkness and dissolving moonlit shadows. The fall night was chilly and the wind blew wildly, so through the mountain passes I fought to steady the truck in the gusts. And though I had been driving along this freeway section for over an hour, few cars crossed me along the way. All was going as I had planned.

Then, looking to my right, I asked, "Are you awake?"

There was no answer, nor any movement, from my passenger. She was lying, eyes closed, with the back of her head resting against the door. I could hear her breathing and saw her chest rise, fall, and rise again. She was dead to the world.

Thus far, she hadn't awoken, and I hoped she would remain deep asleep until I reached the cabin—my destination.

I struggled to keep my attention on the directions and not on her. "Don't miss the exit," I told myself. "It should be coming up."

Soon I exited onto the highway I wanted. Again I looked over at her, but this time I reflected on her face—the young, creamy skin, framed by long, straight, brown hair (the hairline, thick and low, reminded me of a lion's mane), the slender nose (how I liked her nose), the high cheekbones, and the small, round chin. She was still as attractive as I remembered. Even more so, I convinced myself.

"Hey," I said. "You awake?"

Again there was no reply, but I smelled the trace of her gardenia perfume blending with the scent of her sweat.

The sign by the guardrail told me the elevation was 3,000 feet, so I knew the road I was looking out for was just minutes ahead, among the dozens of mountains silhouetted in dark, darker, and darkest grays against the contrasting and illuminated silver-gray sky. I drove on.

About ten miles later, several sighs emanated from my passenger, and then she was quiet again. It was about time she started to rouse, and I considered giving her another injection. If I had to stop where we could be seen, I didn't want her awake, and I didn't want to struggle with her before we got to the cabin.

Upon reaching the road, I turned off the highway and drove west. The mountain base I was heading for was roughly another two hours away, and the summit and cabin an additional thirty minutes farther.

I couldn't believe I had made it that far, and though I was still not relieved, I was feeling slightly more confident because my plan was proceeding smoothly.

"Hell, I bet my life you'll be surprised," I said.

I then began to recall the beginning of this tragedy—though at the time, while driving toward the mountain, I didn't think the night would turn out as tragically as it did. My thoughts went back to that dreadful day, to what had set all this in motion: my coming home two years earlier to an empty house and "the letter," which I had memorized.

*Edgar,*

    *It makes me sick to write this. I don't believe we should be ending our relationship, but I think you were right. There are many things I still want to do before I make an oath to God regarding our life together. I don't think you'll wait, and I don't expect you to.*

    *Virginia*

No "dear." No "good-bye." No "thanks." No "sincerely" or "love." That letter on the dining table was as cold and painful as frostbite, and it had hit me like an avalanche.

Still piloting west toward the mountain, I began to reflect on the night before I discovered the letter.

*I had walked into the bedroom while she was applying sunless tanning lotion to her legs. She got angry and told me to get out. Later I asked her why she was so worried about how her legs looked. She didn't answer but instead asked me if I thought she needed braces. I looked at her teeth and told her that during the three years we had dated, and the past twenty-two months we had lived together, I had enjoyed her smile, had put my tongue in her mouth hundreds of times, and at no time did I ever even notice her lower teeth were even slightly crooked.*

*I knew then what was happening. The writing was on her legs in sunless tanning lotion. There were signs it was coming. There usually are. Frequently they are revealed in dreams, dreams that come from either God communicating or the unconscious mind piecing together the hints, evidence, and implications the conscious mind ignores, denies, doesn't recognize, or just refuses to accept.*

*But when it happens—the separation or breakup—the mind goes into shock, and it suffers.*

*The college she was going to attend had sponsored a week of parties on campus before the semester began, and she hadn't invited me to join her. I had gone to this college six years earlier and knew that guests were welcome at these gatherings. She got mad when I told her that.*

*I also recalled the dozen or so names and telephone numbers she had come home with after the parties. She had even bought a second cell phone during that party week but hadn't given me the number. This I thought peculiar, and it added to my paranoia.*

I stopped recollecting for a moment and looked at her. She still didn't stir, so my mind again drifted back to those events that cursed my existence.

*Two nights before the letter appeared, we talked about our future together over dinner in a cheap restaurant. I told her I wanted some sort of commitment, said I could go on as we were for another year but not for two (which was how long it would take her to finish her degree).*

*I had supported her the entire time we were living together, even though she worked part-time. But with the attention she had been getting from men lately, and the $29,000 check the government had given her to attend that private college, she was acting defiant, contributing little money to our bills, and doing little if any housework.*

*That evening she asked me to shave her legs and pubic hair, which I willingly did, for I had done these, and the many other intimate things she had asked me to do for her, numerous times. At bedtime, she asked if*

*I would read to her while we lay in bed. I read "The Short Happy Life of Francis Macomber." It seemed appropriate——I knew she would hurt me.*

*After I finished the story, she requested a back massage——these readings and massages had become something of a ritual——and the rubdown was followed by almost two hours of foreplay and lovemaking.*

I also remembered vividly how fulfilled I felt when making love to her. It gave me pleasure, something to look forward to, a reason to work hard and make money.

*I whispered, "Can you tell I'm making love and not just having sex?"*

*She answered, "Yes," into my ear, while I licked and kissed her neck passionately and released my deep, guttural purr, the one that told her I was going to give it to her——and good.*

*I kissed her closed eyes, her nose, her ears, and anywhere I thought would arouse her and make her feel wanted and needed.*

*I believed we could somehow connect mentally, or possibly spiritually, if I earnestly made love to her, and I tried my best to show her I loved her while we made love. Just telling her I loved her didn't seem enough. I thought she might not believe me. What is it they say? "Show, don't tell." And I wanted to show her as often as she would allow me.*

*"Don't we look great together?" she said as we faced the mirror, still joined, doggy style, on the bed. "We would make great-looking kids," she added.*

*"Do you want kids?" I asked.*

*"Yes," she said.*

*"With me?"*

*"Yes."*

The truck bumped and jumped as it ran over a hole in the road, and this jarred my thoughts back from the past. Unfortunately, the jolt brought more than just my thoughts to the present: Virginia was beginning to stir.

Then it happened—what made me anxious. I saw her eyes, those mysterious eyes that had at one time had considerable control over me. But no more, I told myself. She would never control me again. As I watched, they slowly closed.

Continuing to drive, I recalled the last time I had seen her eyes: the morning of the day I had come home to a lonely house and found her Dear John letter, which was actually a Dear Edgar letter without the "Dear." *Cowardly bitch*, I thought.

Then I wondered if she saw me when she opened her eyes, if she recognized me. So much time had passed, nearly three years. I supposed she probably never wanted to see my face again. Not because if she did, she would be unable to resist returning to me—which she had told a friend of mine—but more likely because she believed I would strangle her. Of course, this wasn't what crossed my mind.

I heard her shift in her seat. I glanced at her and wondered what she would say when she awoke and saw me. Me. With her. I imagined she would remain silent as fear enveloped her—fear arising from her own guilt, fear from expecting me to seek revenge, fear that I was crazy.

A moment later, her eyes still closed, she began to murmur. I considered remaining silent even if she asked me questions but then decided against it. I didn't want to torture her.

"Welcome back," I said.

She opened her eyes and blinked as her head wobbled slightly from side to side several times. She seemed to ponder where she was. She wasn't completely conscious yet, most likely due to the lingering effects of the drug I had given her.

"What...Where am I?" she finally uttered.

Though it was difficult for me to keep my composure, I remained calm. We hadn't spoken since the morning of "the letter." I wanted to yell and berate her for how she had treated me, used me, wasted my time, and destroyed my life. Damn, after what she put me through, it would have been a just reward if I...

I needed to tell her how horrible my existence had been since she had abandoned me, without even giving me a chance to say good-bye. Oh, how I had grieved—as if she had died, as a loving husband does for his beloved wife who dies unexpectedly and without him.

"No, it can't be!" she said, raising her shaking hands to her face, seeming to recognize me and comprehend the situation she was in.

*It can, and it is*, I thought. But I said nothing and looked straight ahead, watching the turns in the road my headlights revealed.

She appeared to be in shock, too horrified to even scream, and we traveled at least a mile before she spoke again.

"What have you done, Edgar?" she asked warily.

"What have I done?" I shot back, a bit out of control. "What have I done? What have *you* done?"

She didn't answer but jerked back against the door.

"I did what I had to do," I said, and took several deep breaths. The exhales were audible. She must have seen my jaw muscles throb as my teeth clenched because she stared at me and didn't speak for several minutes.

"How long have I been out?" she asked.

*Not long enough*, I thought, for we were still almost two hours from the cabin. She waited. I considered telling her but thought it would just upset her more.

"How did I get here?"

I looked at her, to show her how. *Me,* I thought. *That's how.*

She appeared to understand.

"I remember pulling into my garage and closing the door," she said. "Then...Then...I can't remember after that. Did you—"

"Yes," I said.

"You were waiting for me?"

"I waited a long time."

She tried to sit up. It took her a couple of tries. Then she began looking around, out the windows, as a ground squirrel does when it sticks its head out of a hole and looks for danger.

"Where are we?"

"Where I want us to be," I told her, knowing it would do her no good trying to determine where we were. The mountains we were in looked like many others in that wilderness, and the darkness made it difficult to see anything outside the windows, with only moonlight and headlights to see by. Besides, there were no artificial lights nearby or in the distance, so for all she knew we were in Alaska or Russia or Italy, but certainly not near a city or town of any significant size.

And as for time, she had no idea how long she had been unconscious or how long we had been traveling. For her, it could have been hours, even days.

"Where though?" she asked.

I glared at her for a moment, then looked back at the road.

"Where are you taking me, Edgar?"

She used my name, as if that would change anything—make me warm to her, make me change my mind. I didn't say a word or look at her. She didn't deserve my pity or my attention.

"You're not going to tell me?" she asked after a minute or so.

I shook my head.

"What…What are you going to do with me?"

This time I looked at her.

"Edgar," she said. "What are you going to do?"

"I'll do what I have to do," I said, glaring at her.

"Stop! *Please* stop! Stop now!" she shouted.

I didn't. I was keeping to the plan.

*"Stop!"* she screamed.

"No!" I yelled. "*You* stop!"

"Stop! Stop! Stop!" she cried out.

I knew then I had made a mistake, not giving her another injection when she had begun to revive. She was hysterical, and I needed to do something.

"Stop, or else!" I shouted, reaching into my coat pocket and pulling out a syringe. I held it out toward her, and she pressed herself against the door, with her eyes, those dark and powerful eyes, bulging from their sockets. She didn't scream again.

"I'm going to be sick," she said.

"Be sick," I said.

"Please, Edgar...for God's sake."

"For God's sake?" I said. "Why for His sake? Why not for your sake or for mine? Besides, God doesn't get involved."

"Please pull over. My stomach is killing me."

I assumed the drug's side effects were probably making her nauseous. Besides, eleven hours had passed since I had drugged her and laid her in my truck, so she had been without food or water. With that in mind and the possibility of her having motion sickness from driving through bumpy and twisting mountain roads, I didn't doubt she was feeling ill.

"All right!" I yelled, and began looking for a place to park, knowing it was most likely another mistake to stop before reaching the cabin, to deviate from my plan.

But it was too late. She began to retch.

"Here," I said, throwing her the sweater that was on the front seat. "Vomit in this."

She did, *"Uhhhgggttt! Uhhhgggttt!"* and although not much liquid came up, the smell was putrid.

"Jesus Christ!" I blurted.

I opened my window to let in fresh air. It swished against the window channel and door body. It was cool and smelled like Christmas—fresh evergreens.

She retched again.

An open area appeared on the right, so I turned off the road and into the glade, which spread out for about a hundred yards. I drove across the grassy clearing until I came to the edge of the woods, where large conifers loomed like columns in a Gothic church. She looked surprised and scared that I had driven in so far. I supposed she knew that anything could happen. Anything.

As I slowed the truck to a stop and shut off the engine and headlights, she became deathly still. But the strong wind that rocked the truck whooshed and whistled its hymn through the open window. While the boughs and branches swayed from the gusts, shadows wavered inside and outside the truck, and the blue moon, full and bright, bathed the undulating grasses in silvery light.

What happened next was no surprise: she started pulling on the door handle, struggling desperately to get out, to no avail. Frustrated, she beat on the door with her hands.

"It's no use," I said, glaring at her. "I disconnected the lock."

Her hands immediately dropped to her sides, her chin collapsed to her chest, and she began to sob.

It was then that I noticed, as I peered through the windshield, an opening into the woods, with several cedars standing like sentinels on each side of the entrance. And something moved: a shadow near the opening. I was certain of it. Something had emerged from the large hole in the woods.

"Did you see that?" I asked.

She lifted her head, controlling her sobbing.

"See what?" she asked, jerking her head to look out one window and then another. "What is it?"

"I'm not sure."

"Close your window," she said, frightened.

As I did so, I observed more shapes moving outside the void in the woods—animals of some kind.

"We're not alone," I said.

"Oh my God, what's there?"

I had stopped the truck under the limb of a large fir, and as I looked through the window, the dark figures began to move away from the creepy opening. Holding my breath, I saw several of them dart out into the open gray and then back into the covered, black shade, their noses shifting high into the air and back along the ground as they moved.

"Wolves!" I said.

She gasped and stiffened.

"They must have arrived when we stopped," I said. "They know we're here, and they're inspecting us. Who knows what would have happened if you had gotten out?"

"For Christ's sake, let's get out of here!" she cried.

"Don't worry," I said. "They can't hurt us in here."

"Oh, God, help me!" she cried.

"Don't rely on Him," I told her. "How many nights and days did I cry and pray to Him to bring you back to me? I didn't go to work for weeks. I tried. I really did. Overwhelmed with grief and panic, I sought relief in any church I could find, dozens of them over many weeks. But it didn't help. My prayers weren't answered, and I didn't find comfort. So some nights I prayed to the moon. I would drive up into the hills, stop on a dark, quiet road, alone with 'the man in the moon,' and pray. Oh, how I prayed! Sometimes on my knees, in the dirt. But I never even received a call from you. Nothing."

I looked away from her and let out a short, sarcastic laugh.

"Turn on the headlights," she urged. "I can't see them."

"That might attract attention," I said, "*unwanted* attention."

"At least start the engine," she pleaded. "It might scare them off."

"I told you not to worry."

"Don't worry?"

"I have protection."

"What?" she asked, snapping her head toward me.

I waited a second, then reached my left hand down under the seat. I slowly pulled up a shiny, black object. She didn't appear to know what it was until she straightened up and pushed herself back into the door. She knew. She said nothing, but her breath quickened and her eyes widened with fear.

"Oh, this?" I said, turning the revolver as it reflected the moonlight. "Don't let this scare you. It's for protection. Those are wolves. They kill."

"I'm frightened, Edgar."

"Why?" I asked. "Don't you trust me?"

She hesitated for a moment.

"Why am I here, Edgar? Why?" she asked pitifully. "What do you want from me?"

"To talk," I said, putting the gun back under the seat. "It's been a long time since we talked."

She paused.

"About what, Edgar?" she asked. "Do you know what you've done?"

I didn't answer.

"You know they'll be looking for me."

"Who? Who will be looking for you?" I asked. "Who knows you're gone? Who knows where you are?"

Her shoulders slumped and her head tilted forward. She must have known I was right.

"So...what will you do now?" she asked.

"Why not just wait for 'whoever' to find you?"

"Please, don't be like that. There must be something I can say to—"

"To what? What the hell are you going to say," I asked, "to make everything okay? Everything will *not* be okay!"

"Please, Edgar...you said...we were going to talk. I want to...talk," she said, stumbling over her words.

I took in a couple of slow, deep breaths and exhaled them loudly.

"So, what shall we talk about?" I asked.

"Whatever you want."

"On second thought, maybe we shouldn't," I said. "Now isn't the time. We'll only end up fighting."

"No. I don't want to fight. I never want to fight. Please let's not fight. I just want to go back."

"We can't go back now," I said.

"But why?"

"I need time."

"Time for what, Edgar?"

"Time to think...or whatever," I blurted out.

"Are you going to kill me?"

The question seemed absurd—I once loved this woman. But there it was, hanging like a noose over her head. Then I asked myself, *Are you going to kill her?*

I looked into her eyes. I wanted to feel again, to have compassion, to love her, but the stone in my chest remained cold and solid.

"Of course not," I answered a few moments later. And I answered truthfully.

"I'm sorry I hurt you," she said. "I didn't want to hurt you. Believe me, I never wanted things to turn out the way they did."

"I believe you."

"I know how you feel, but—"

"You have *no idea* how I feel," I interrupted, indignant.

"You're right…You're right. I'm sorry," she said. "But imagine how *I'm* feeling."

"It's not my fault," I said.

"I know it's not your fault," she said. "It's nobody's fault. It just happens."

"*It's not my fault.*"

"Please, can we go somewhere else?" she asked, looking through the window. "This place scares me."

I thought for a minute and decided it was best if I got her to the cabin as soon as possible. I had already taken too many chances, and things were no longer proceeding as I had planned.

"Yes," I said, nodding my head and starting the engine. When the headlights shone and the tires flung up the soil, the pack scattered back into the shadows.

Soon we were on the road again, with the dark figures of the evergreens, lashed by the wind, looking strong and impenetrable on both sides, like sentries guarding the woods from intruders. The road looked much narrower. I hadn't noticed the gradual squeezing in of the woods before we stopped.

"Where are we going now?" she asked, pressed against her door and fumbling to get the seat belt snapped. "Edgar?"

"I heard you."

"Can you tell me where we're going?"

"Not now," I said.

"How about where we are?"

"I'll tell you where we are when we get there."

"Okay, Edgar."

"Listen, I'm sorry. I'm confused and nervous, and you're not making things easier by asking so many questions. Just sit back and try to calm yourself. We'll be there soon."

Then I observed a weird and eerie phenomenon, an expanse of tumbling, black clouds advancing swiftly across the gray sky like a swarm of locusts. It soon eclipsed the glowing moon and darkened the sky and everything around us. I lowered my window to get a better view and felt a peculiar energy in the air, what seemed to be an electric charge that stimulated the hairs on my body.

*CRACK!!*

A dazzling bolt of white lightning splintered the dark sky and struck just up the road, producing a bright white burst. I jumped in my seat, and Virginia yelped. The jagged traces and blinding flash lingered in my vision for several seconds.

"We're safe in the truck," I said.

"Are you sure?"

"The tires ground us. We're fine."

I then saw an orange and red flame where the white burst had been, about a quarter of a mile away. A tree on the side of the road was burning. When we reached it, we saw that its top half had fallen across the road and that the trunk was smoking. It was an unnerving sight.

"We can't get by," she said.

"We'll get by," I said.

Though I had a power saw in the back of the truck, along with other supplies—two spare tires, two large cans of gasoline, a tool box, spare hoses and belts, and food—I didn't want to waste any time or risk being seen cutting the tree to get by it, there being a chance someone (a forest ranger, game warden, hunter, even a camper) might see us. So I searched the roadside, thinking I could weave the truck between the trees and bypass the fallen one.

"We'll go around," I said, shifting the truck into four-wheel drive and steering off the road. Snaking through the trees, I came upon a small clearing. Just then I noticed the red light on my dash, indicating the truck was low on gas, so I decided to stop so I could tend to Virginia and fill the tank. I killed the engine and headlights.

Another lightning bolt struck nearby with a tremendous crack. Thinking a rainstorm was looming, I raised my window but left a two-inch gap.

"I'm going to put gas in the tank. Stay put."

I took the gun from under the seat and placed it between my pants and waist, then reached behind the seat, grabbed the large flashlight and flipped it on. I got out of the truck, re-trieved a gas can from the back, and began filling the tank. A couple of minutes later, Virginia moved over to the driver's seat and said something through the gap in the window.

"What?" I was at the back of the truck and couldn't hear her. I walked to the door and opened it.

"I said, I need to pee!"

"You can hold it for a while."

"How long is a while?"

"It's just that, a while," I said sarcastically.

"Go straight to hell," she said abruptly.

"I can't," I said. "I'll probably get a tour of heaven first, to see what I'll be missing."

"Oh, please, Edgar. I'm sorry," she said. "I didn't mean that."

"Just get out and do what you have to do."

"Are you going to hurt me if I get out?"

"Should I?" I answered. After a moment, I added, "Of course not. Would I have gone to all this trouble if I were going to hurt you?"

"I need a light."

"Hold on," I said. "I have another one in the back." I fin-ished pouring the gas, returned the empty can to the back of the truck, and grabbed the other flashlight.

"Here," I said, handing it to her.

"Will this give enough light?" she asked. "I don't want any wolves to come around."

"There are no animals here," I told her.

"How can you be sure?"

"Well then, just do your business here," I said, pointing to the ground next to the truck.

"No, I'll just walk a ways."

"As long as I can see you," I cautioned.

"It's so dark," she said.

Then I figured that anyone driving past us would see the light from the flashlights as easily as they would the headlights. Besides, it was unlikely anyone would be traveling on this road at two in the morning.

"Okay, I'll put on the headlights for a minute or two. They certainly won't come around with the headlights on."

"Are you sure?"

"Hell, I'm standing outside here; there are no wolves."

"You'll watch me, right?"

"Just stay in the light where I can see you."

I reached into the cab and switched on the headlights, and the barren ground lit up before us. Virginia looked and listened as she sat at the open door.

"Remember. Stay in the light," I told her again, though I felt she was too afraid to run and hide. Anyway, I knew I could catch her, and she would be sorry.

She grabbed the flashlight, switched it on, and stepped out of the truck, stumbling a few steps as she tried to walk. She stopped and looked around, then staggered about twenty feet to the center of the clearing.

As I watched her let down her pants and squat, another close crack of thunder rumbled, and as if by sorcery, the headlights went out.

A moment later, a grayish haze appeared all around us, and I noticed the glowing moon again as the ominous, black clouds receded as quickly as they had come.

Then something caught my attention at the edge of the woods. I stared harder and saw shadows moving among the trees. And out of the darkness, something treaded out from between two large pines and stopped between Virginia and the truck. It was a beast, and it was standing on its rear legs—like a man.

I inhaled a deep breath, petrified before the hairy figure. Unable to scream, my heart pounding, my eyes protruding, I gazed up in awe at the tall beast. It glared down at me, its silver eyes reflecting the light of the blue moon. *My God*, he was flesh, standing long limbed, large pawed, broad chested, and with a head that looked too large for his body. Barely a couple of yards separated us, and behind him were his menacing minions: large black wolves, fierce and growling, advancing slowly toward their praying prey—Virginia.

They surrounded her but were tentative, as if awaiting a command...from their *lord*.

I seized the gun from my waist and pointed.

Virginia shrieked, "Edgar! *I don't want to die!*"

I didn't fire.

"Edgar! For heaven's sake, *please!*" she screeched, with a horror that stiffened my heart and stopped my blood cold. I gasped, dropped the gun, and fell backward onto my palms and ass, but my eyes didn't leave the gaze of *my* mysterious intruder. And even as I expected him to leap upon me and rip into my body with his bared canines, the beast remained motionless.

Then it struck me that I had seen this creature before—during a blue moon two years earlier—when I was praying in the mountains, alone, with only that moon for company and hope.

*Back then I was yelling and cursing God and the saints and angels for not helping me, for allowing me to feel so lonely and useless, for me needing someone, anyone, to listen, to understand, to feel for me, pity me—pitiful me. All my muscles were tensed, and I could feel the veins in my neck and see those on my forearms bulging.*

*A thought came to me, and being frantic, I acted on it. I started asking for help and intervention from…I wasn't myself. Something strange was happening to me: my mind became foggy, and my body went numb. I began to hallucinate, or I assumed I was hallucinating. At the time, I believed it was my imagination or perhaps the peculiar chemicals in my body—generated by stress and depression—that were causing visions and delusions.*

*Then it was there. In front of me stood a beast, the beast—the same beast that I now beheld. It was staring at me. Terrified, I trembled as it stepped closer. I dropped to my knees and prayed for help. Oh, not the way I had prayed most of my life to God, but to this thing, this being, this creature that stood before me.*

*Then, somehow, I knew that it was real and that it would help me. It was able to communicate this to me without words or visible signs. But I knew. Or I thought I knew, because I wasn't sure if I was imagining the whole encounter, this silent communication between us, or even if the beast was actually there. So I prayed as hard as I knew how, or could, to get Virginia back. I wanted to get her back, and I asked the beast to do it for me.*

*And I suppose it did. It got her back. Oh, did it ever get her back! It got her back for me not in the way my conscious mind had wished—to have her come back into my life—but the way my subconscious mind wanted—to get her back through revenge.*

*And what did I give the beast in return? At the time, I somehow felt it had taken pity on me because I had given it something it thought mysterious: tears. Oh, not the tears that result from a grain of sand or dust getting into the eye, or from physical pain, but tears that come from thoughts, the effects of mental anguish, heartbreak, disappointment, loss—emotional tears, the most mysterious things in the universe.*

*And then the beast was gone. I had looked down to where my tears had wet the ground, and when I looked up it was not there. I never saw it or even thought about it again, as unlikely as that seems, until it reappeared between Virginia and me.*

"What are you doing on this mountain with us?" I asked the beast standing before me. He just stared at me.

I felt dizzy, then my head began to ache, and somehow I knew that my mind was being molested, violated, raped. The sensation was alien to me, yet knowable and expected. The beast had entered my mind, knew my thoughts. *You! You!* I thought. *You can read my mind. You know what I'm thinking.* "My God!" I cried.

The assault lasted several minutes, it seemed, before my faculties returned and I heard Virginia wailing my name, "Ed—gar! *Ed—gar!*" dragging out each anguished syllable.

Her screams shattered my soul, for I knew what would happen to her, encircled as she was by at least six of the demonic wolves, knew they would kill her.

Then, as if she had resigned herself to her fate, she stopped screaming, and I saw the demons lunge toward her, their teeth bared and glinting from the moon's rays. I heard no further supplications from her, only the growls from her attackers, the sounds of tearing clothing, and the snaps, cracks, and rips of Virginia's flesh, bones, and sinews.

My mind began to dissolve as I watched the last thing I saw—his eyes—those possessing eyes that looked to hold the secret to man's existence, that seemed to invite me into its thoughts, to be thanking me for something—I knew not what. I blacked out, or perhaps the beast forced me unconscious as he melded with my mind.

I awoke at dawn, not knowing how long I had been lying there, and not sure if what rushed into my memory had been just a terrifying nightmare. After getting to my feet, breathing deeply, and waiting for my dexterity to return and my equilibrium to stabilize, I looked for Virginia, or what I thought might remain of her.

In the clearing where I believed the attack had occurred, I found neither her nor anything that was from her or of her. I called out loudly, "Virginia! Virginia!" And then, as I looked down, a ruddy color seized my attention. Mixed with the pine needles was blood, some already dried to brown.

Horrified, I began to curse God and the saints in heaven because I knew for certain that Virginia was dead and that I was damned.

---

It wasn't long before the FBI tracked me down, thanks to all those video cameras mounted at intersections and all along the freeways. I also made it easy for them. They found my gun right where I had left it, in my truck, along with the syringes and traces of Virginia's blood, which I probably got on me when I had looked for her on that horrific morning.

They never found her body, though. They searched in pits, under floors, and behind walls, but they didn't find her. They couldn't. She was nowhere to be found. She was gone.

But they institutionalized me anyway. And as I sit here now, in my hospital room, reflecting on what I've written, I know my story happened. I'm no writer who can make this up. I didn't kill her. I know I didn't kill her. I am not crazy.

# A RANK ABOVE

F ROM A TREE limb, high above the grass, they watched the men playing football in the park.

"They don't look like I expected," said one.

"Yeah, I'm not impressed," said the other, watching the men form two lines to face each other. "I don't see why they're so special."

"Actually, they look kind of weak to me," said the first, as one man hiked the ball to another.

"They're definitely not as strong as we are," said the second, watching the men run.

"Should we challenge them to see what they're really made of?" asked the first, seeing a man throw the ball into the air.

"I don't think that's a good idea," replied the second. "We might get into trouble."

"Maybe no one knows we're here," said the first.

"They always know where we are," said the second. "*Always*."

"I know. You're right. But I'd still like to compete against them," said the first, watching two men jump to catch the ball. "We've traveled a long distance to get here."

"You can see they're no match for us," said the second, watching as two men chased the one who had caught the ball. "They don't even fly."

"They don't even move fast," said the first, as one man tackled the other with the ball.

"But they do invent some interesting things," said the second.

"Interesting for them but not so interesting compared to what we see and know," said the first, seeing a man help another to his feet.

"Still, they've come a long way since their beginning," said the second.

"And yet they're not as advanced as we are, by far," said the first.

"But they are ranked above us," said the second.

"Yeah, why is that?" asked the first, seeing one man pat another's back. "Why *are* they ranked above us?"

"It's because they're weaker than us," replied the second. "They don't have our abilities. They must work hard for what they have…struggle just to survive briefly before they die. All of them die. But mostly because, unlike us, they must earn their positions—and not all of them get one."

"It's not by my choosing that they have it tougher than us and that they're vulnerable," said the first. "I'm not God."

"It really doesn't matter much to me where we're ranked," said the second. "We have everything we need or want."

"I guess you're right," said the first. "Besides, I wouldn't want to trade places with them."

"Nor would I," said the second. "I like being an angel."

"Me too."

"Shall we go?"

"I'll race you back to heaven!"

# DUCK OR DOLL

MARY RAN OUT the kitchen door. There was the sharp slam of the screen door, quickly followed by the slapping of her leather-soled shoes over the wood flooring of the porch and the expected squeaking of the front steps.

"Bye, Mother!"

"Mary, where are you going?" her mother called out of a window.

"I'm going to the store and then to the library," Mary said.

"Be sure to be back by dark, darling," said her mother.

"Oh, I'll be back before dinner, Mother. Don't worry."

"You know how your father gets when you're late for dinner, Mary."

Having scampered away from the house, the young girl was already too far away to clearly hear her mother's last admonishment.

She was hurrying to see the new dolls imported from Europe that the town's general store had received the previous day. She had purchased at least half a dozen of these beautiful dolls from the storekeeper over the past two years. The gentle, old woman, knowing Mary liked to collect and play with them, informed Mary of the order six weeks earlier and reminded her only two days ago of its due delivery the following day.

Now on this spring afternoon, the weather was sunny and warm, and Mary felt the sun's rays caressing her porcelain skin. Yet the sky was filled with white and gray clouds, and she discerned numerous characters and objects sprouting from these heavenly billows. She envisaged angels throwing giant cotton balls into the wind. Possibly they were racing them, seeing who could send one across the vast sky first.

The mild breeze had picked up, and she felt her sateen dress tugging on her as the wind made it billow like a sail, and smelled the aroma of the cherry blossoms growing near the pond next to her house that the gusts seized and carried to her nose.

Strolling down the worn and narrow path that weaved past the pond, she headed towards the apple orchard that separated the town of Pleasant View from her family's property. She heard the crackling and scratching of thousands of apple leaves as the wind rustled them and her golden hair into a frenzy.

She arrived where the path divided the orchard from the pond and the grass grew knee-high. She listened to the reeds along the water rubbing and hissing as undulating ripples, pushed by flurries, glided through them. Then while passing some bushes and glancing down so as not to trip across a branch or rock, she noticed something beside a leafy, green bush. It appeared to be a small white object. Deciding to take a closer look, she cautiously stepped off the path and into the grass. Several feet away she came upon the intriguing item.

It was indeed small but not white as she first had thought. Rather, it was a waxy, creamy color, and certainly an egg. She looked around the surrounding bushes and grass for some indication as to where it could have come from. Nothing clued her in to its origin. She thought for a minute that it might be a turtle egg. *Turtles lay eggs, and there are snapping turtles in the pond*, she thought. She knelt, resolved to touch the curious item. It was pleasantly smooth and warm. Then, just as her hand clutched the egg, a piercing screech from above startled her. Anxious, she peered up and beheld a grand, brown eagle circling in the sky.

"Wow!" she cried. "An eagle egg!"

This blurting out startled the two ducks paddling among the reeds to her right. She identified them instantly as wood ducks: the male with its iridescent, green- and white-feathered head, and its red-encircled eyes: the female with its predominantly brown plumage and white-patched eyes. Beating their wings and crying out *cre-eeek, cre-eeek, cre-eeek*, they swam closer to her.

Then two large and strikingly beautiful white birds, floating serenely about seven yards out from where she was kneeling, also caught her attention. They had long, slender necks that curved gracefully up towards their shy heads. *Swans*!

*How pretty they are*, she thought, and back her focus shifted to the helpless little egg lying between her legs. She reached over to her side and opened the little pink purse hanging from her shoulder. Taking out a soft handkerchief, she then gently picked up and wrapped the precious egg, and placed it into her purse. In seconds, she was back on her feet and walking briskly towards the town, which she could see up ahead.

It was not far off, no more than a quarter of a mile down the path. She regarded the vibrant, verdant woods that covered the mountain range beyond the town. They appeared to be patches of green hair growing from the earth's skin. *I wonder if the mother eagle is perched in one of those tall pine trees, watching us*, she thought. She hoped the magnificent eagle would fly over her again so she could get a better look at it and know what to expect from the egg that she was carrying because she had already decided to hatch and raise the bird herself.

She thought that with her father's help she could teach the eagle to catch rabbits for them. Then she thought about how cute the ones around her house were, how often they amused her with their chasing each other about, jumping over one another, and making delightful designs in the snow. *Anyway, we don't eat rabbit*, she thought.

She imagined her new responsibility would be strong and handsome, that it would dive faster than the wind. People from the town would admire it and come to her house to watch it fly—to and from her arms. It would be her best friend. How happy and proud these thoughts made her feel!

Then she began to worry that she knew nothing about taking care of an egg or raising a fledgling eagle. *What will I feed it? Where will I keep it?* She supposed she would need a large cage, or perhaps she would have to tie twine to the eaglet's leg to prevent it from flying away. Then she thought old Mrs. Potter, at the general store, would have something to help her, so she quickened her pace.

Minutes later, she reached the town and walked from the path to Main Street. Mrs. Potter's store was just a block up, on the other side of the street.

In her excitement, Mary covered the four steps to the entrance with only two bounds. Mrs. Potter, who had turned towards the front door when its small bell tinkled, greeted Mary as she entered.

"Good afternoon, Mary. I suppose you're here to pick up a new doll to add to your wonderful collection." Mrs. Potter had little doubt about Mary's reason for stopping by her store so was surprised to hear the young girl's response.

"No, Mrs. Potter, I'm not."

Then Mary glanced to her right. Before the store's front window stood a magnificent arrangement of at least a dozen wonderful dolls from France. Mrs. Potter, who had owned the store for over twenty years, knew how to display her important items. She had arranged the dolls sitting and standing before a decorative toy fireplace. Miniature walls separated the dolls' home from the small ceramic houses that filled the background, giving the impression the dolls were in a home set in a quaint little town, one much like Pleasant View.

Mary fixed her attention on an angelic doll with golden hair and blue eyes, similar to her own. Its white dress and the tiny book it held in its porcelain hands made Mary smile. She knew this doll was the one she would buy. She reached into her little pink purse to assure herself she had the money she had saved from her birthday two months earlier, but upon looking at the bundled handkerchief, she remembered the egg.

Once again, Mary told Mrs. Potter that she was there for a reason other than buying a doll. "No doll, Mrs. Potter. I need your help with something else."

Mrs. Potter was now quite curious to know why Mary had come.

"What can I help you with, child?"

"Well, I found this," said Mary, opening her purse and carefully retrieving the small bundle.

Mrs. Potter looked on anxiously, eager to see what could be more important to her familiar customer than a new doll.

Mary placed the wrapped cloth onto the counter, next to the register, and proceeded to open it with great care, as if expecting something to jump out. When the oval orphan appeared, Mary looked up into Mrs. Potter's round, red-cheeked face and said, "It's an *eagle* egg."

Mrs. Potter, though somewhat relieved, was still surprised to see the cause of Mary's concern.

"Why, it just may be," said Mrs. Potter, who had seen thousands of chicken eggs in her time. But this one did not look like any chicken egg she could recall. It was bigger than a chicken egg, yet not as big as…"Where did you find it?"

"By our pond."

"I see."

"I don't know what to do," said Mary. "But I'll try to take good care of it. Can you please help me, Mrs. Potter?"

"There, there, child," said Mrs. Potter. "Don't get yourself all worried about what we can take care of."

"I have my birthday money in my purse. I can buy whatever you tell me I need," said Mary, opening her purse to show the folded bills to Mrs. Potter.

"I have just what you need. I'll be back in a jiffy," said Mrs. Potter, disappearing through the curtain hanging over the doorway behind her.

Now Mrs. Potter, having served the townspeople for many years, had seen her share of children wanting to hatch eggs. Some tried to hatch store-bought chicken eggs straight from a container or refrigerator, while other children—in their infinite wandering, searching, and hunting for anything to occupy their time, having actually obtained healthy and maturing eggs, most of them from the woods and waters surrounding the town—attempted to hatch viable ones. As a result, she had learned to keep a few essentials handy to help the children hatch their eggs at home. The two most important ones were heat lamps and shoeboxes.

While Mrs. Potter searched her back room, Mary heard boxes sliding and chair legs dragging against the concrete floor, then the sounds of rummaging and muttering. She specifically heard, "I know it must be here somewhere. I had two of them left." This was soon followed by clattering and then "Saint Peter, here's one!"

Mrs. Potter reentered the storefront and took her place behind the counter. Her face was flushed from her exertions, in particular from bending over and pushing boxes, which had caused the blood to rush to her head. Her hair was also askew, and she reached up and positioned what steamed-in curls she could back into their previous places.

"Here we are, child." She placed a small heat lamp upon the counter for Mary to admire.

"What is it?" exclaimed Mary, looking at the plug and its attached light, thinking it could be used as a nightlight for her new baby. *They're probably afraid of the dark, like I was when I was younger*, she thought.

"It's a heat lamp, Mary. You must keep the egg warm in order for it to hatch." And reaching down and bringing up a shoebox, she said, "Here's a box you can fill with a towel and some cotton. It should make a nice makeshift nest for the youngster to keep warm in."

Delighted, Mary smiled and rose up and down on her toes. She would take good care of the baby, as if it were her own child. It would grow to be the most magnificent eagle in the sky.

"Now, Mary," said Mrs. Potter, patting Mary's hand. "It won't be easy to care for this little angel once it hatches. You'll have to take on the responsibility of being its parent until its old enough to go off on its own. You'll need to show it gentleness, patience, and understanding. And if you don't have much patience now, child, you'll learn some."

Mary was filled with joy. She would be a mother to the eagle.

"Don't worry, Mrs. Potter. I'll take good care of my baby. And it won't have to worry about going off on its own because I will keep it forever!"

"Yes, of course you will, child," was all Mrs. Potter said. But in the back her mind, she knew the snatched life would die, not even hatch.

"How much do I owe you?"

"Nothing."

"Nothing?"

"Nothing...for my favorite customer."

Mary wrapped the egg and returned it to her purse. Then she picked up the box and lamp, and headed for the door. "Thanks, Mrs. Potter."

But as she approached the dolls displayed before the window, she paused and stared at the blond one—for just a moment. Then she opened the door and vanished.

# THE PAYMENT

A s he drove his car, he knew he would get away with what he was planning, the first deed anyway, his purpose. But one way or another, he would not escape—he would have to pay. The police would find him, he thought. But when? How long would it take? And would it be too late; would he be gone too—dead?

It had rained earlier in the evening, but now the black sky drizzled on and off, and the damp streets and sidewalks shined from the streetlights. He glanced at the clock on the dash. *Past one already*, he thought. He drove on, turning his head left and right, looking, spotting someone, but not the man he sought. The front windows were down, and he could hear the hum and splash of the tires whirring over the dank streets as the foul-smelling dampness enveloped him.

"Where are you, you son of a bitch?" he whispered.

He continued to think about this man and the outcomes the night might bring. Would anyone care if this parasite disappeared? Would even his mother miss such a beastly son? His friends, who earned a living from his dealings, might briefly regret his demise, but they would soon find other bastards to work for, or venture out on their own, become street bosses in their turn. In any case, they would not talk to the police.

And would the police even waste men and resources trying to find the one who did what he planned to do to this man, this disease, this infestation? The rat probably had enough enemies on the force that the officers would not even investigate if something tragic happened to him—at least not thoroughly. Some of them might even know the man well enough to want him gone. Getting rid of this man would benefit the city.

Besides, who would even know about the man's departure? It would likely not even get into the newspapers. In this city, Los Angeles, things like it happened almost daily.

Yes, he might get away with even more than he had planned. But even then, he would not have long. "Six to eight months," he remembered them telling him, just six to eight months. *How much time is left?* he pondered. *How much valuable time has passed?*

He turned right at a light and proceeded for half a block. He spotted a man in front of a motel. But he was not the one he was searching for. *Wait…that is him.* The man was talking on a cell phone and gesturing into the air as if he were arguing. The driver nearly slammed on his brakes. *Okay, keep calm and keep driving*, he thought.

"Damn it!" he heard the man yell into the phone. He drove another half block, slowed down, shut off his headlights, and turned into the large parking lot across the street from the motel. Hoping the man did not see him, he parked under a tree about a hundred feet from the street, out of the light but still in sight of the man.

He watched and waited. *So what if he saw me? I'm just a stranger to him.* He could see the man pacing back and forth, talking on the phone and flailing his hands. *He didn't notice me.*

He waited to be sure that the man was alone, that he had not posted his crew nearby. What felt like an hour passed, but was actually only twenty minutes. An occasional car drove by, even a teen on a bike, but there were no pedestrians walking by the motel.

Now so close to his aim, the driver's breathing began to quicken and his thighs started to shake. He gripped the steering wheel to prevent his hands from trembling. *Relax...Breathe.* He closed his eyes and inhaled a couple of deep breaths. *You can do this...You know this is for the best.*

A few more cars passed by. Under the streetlight, the man continued to pace and to brandish his arms. Then a car stopped at the corner. The man halted, the phone still pressed to his ear. A girl stepped out from the passenger door, closed it, and the car sped away.

From the parking lot, the driver had a clear view and knew instantly that she belonged to the man, that he owned her.

She stood in the street, looking at something in her hands, and heard the man whistle to her. She stepped onto the sidewalk, put what she was holding into her small purse, and walked toward him. In high heels and tight shorts, she exaggerated the sway of her expensive legs and backside with purpose.

Then the driver thought of another girl that the man he was watching had owned, a girl he had met one evening while he read a book in a coffee shop. A girl he had liked, that he had paid for—more than once. A girl he had enjoyed and eventually cared for. A girl who had called him from a hospital thirteen weeks ago, because she had nobody else to call, after someone had beaten her to within an inch of her life and disfigured her face. A girl who had died, but not before she had told him who had put her in the hospital: the man with the phone.

He would make the man pay for hurting that girl—someone's daughter, perhaps someone's sister. He would make the man, who had been paid a lot for a long time, pay more than he could ever afford. *Both of us will pay*, he thought.

While the driver recalled all this, he watched the man and girl talking on the sidewalk. She took a phone from her purse and placed a call. A few minutes later, a car with several men in it pulled up to them. She got into the car, and it drove away.

*Ah, there they are*, he thought. *She warned me about them.* Talking to her during those many hours and days at the hospital, he had learned from her what he needed to know for this night: when and how the man conducted his business and on what streets he could find him. She had also told him to be careful because even when the man seemed to be alone on the streets, he usually had a car at the ready with at least two men in it just blocks away. And these men usually kept guns—not in their car, in case the police stopped them, but hidden where the man did business. An emergency call from the man could get his men to his aid in several minutes.

The man himself also kept a gun nearby, in the event someone was stupid enough to confront him on a street. He was cautious, did not like strangers approaching him, and did not conduct transactions in the open. Even his girls did not hand over the money they earned from johns directly to him but would call for the crew, in their car, to rendezvous with them on a side street or in a parking lot.

It was time. *Time to make things right.*

The driver looked around again to make sure no cars or people were coming. Keeping his eyes on the man, he popped the trunk lid, slowly got out of the car and closed the door. From the trunk, he took out a coat and slipped it on. He lowered the lid but did not close it or make a sound. Then he started walking toward the man.

He reached the street before the man noticed him. The man froze and stared at the oncoming stranger. There was no "Who are you?" or "What the hell do you want?" from the man. The driver kept walking, confidently and directly, while peering into the man's eyes. The man appeared to sense that this stranger approaching him, on this deserted street at this time of night, was there for business—grave business.

Now ten feet away from the man, the driver reached into his coat and drew a revolver. It was then that the man appeared to realize that *Death* was there to collect. He turned and ran, trying to dial his phone, but a bullet hit him in the left side. He let out a yelp and dropped the phone but kept on running, clutching his side. He veered into the alley behind the motel and dashed to the trash container. Reaching under it, he yanked out a pistol, but before he could raise the gun above his waist, a second bullet struck his right shoulder. He dropped the gun and collapsed to the ground.

The driver was now looming over him.

"Why are you doing this?" the man asked the stranger.

"I have cancer," the driver replied.

Then...*BANG!*

Neither man heard the shot, but one lay dead, while the other gazed at a body that would never again hurt anyone.

"God forgive me," the driver said, slowly putting the revolver back into his coat. He walked to his car. With sirens howling in the distance, he opened the trunk, took off his coat, threw it into the trunk, closed the lid, got into his car, and drove away.

By dawn, he was in Las Vegas.

# A CRAPPY STORY

W E WERE THE only ones watching a late movie in the theater on a Tuesday evening when I felt the pressure to take a shit, the turd *gopher holing* from my anus.

"I have to use the men's room," I said to her.

So from my seat, I jumped to my feet and ran down the hall and into the restroom where I entered a stall and locked its door. Dropping my pants, I then squatted over the toilet, not bothering to use a seat cover, and shot the cork out. The crap sprayed like champagne. There was farting and squirting sounds, and a nasty methane smell. I groaned.

I knew I had spotted the inside of the bowl with brown bits of poo. I looked. Confirmation. I strained and moaned, and more spraying and dripping and stinking occurred. Relief.

I waited to be sure I was empty. Satisfied I was finished, I pulled a long line of toilet tissue and wrapped it into a loose roll around my right fingers. Then I raised my ass off the seat, reached around with my hand and wiped, smearing soft residue off my orifice. I looked at the wad. Verification.

I repeated the pulling, wrapping, and wiping. It took three more times to assure myself that I would not stain my white undershorts—almost no brown streaks on the paper. I sighed.

I depressed the handle and flushed most of the brown down the drain: most but not all, spots on the toilet rim remained—as did the kimchi smell. I rushed to pull up my pants, buckle my belt, and exit the stall. Quickly I washed my hands. Out of the restroom I ran, down the hall, into the theater, and back to my seat.

"How did it go?" she asked me.

"Fine," I said. "A good story."

"Story?" she asked.

"Yeah, it had a beginning, an activating incident, a climax, an ending, and a denouement."

"You're taking this writing thing a little too far," she said.

"You think?" I said.

"What do you think? Taking a crap is not a story."

"Urinals are displayed as art in museums. Why not a story about taking a shit?"

"Watch the movie, you weirdo," she told me.

# A MAN'S BEST FRIEND

"*Now I lay me down to sleep. I pray the Lord my soul to keep. If I should die before I wake, I pray the Lord my soul to take.*"

The time was 10:57 p.m. when Justin laid his head onto his pillow to sleep.

The barks were loud and continuous.

"Ruff. Ruff. Ruff. Ruff."

He heard them.

*What dog? Whose dog? Certainly a dog.*

Then it was quiet.

His eyes remained closed as his thoughts shaped gray images in the black expanse of his mind. Lying face up, he felt his chest lift and lower with each of his breaths. His left index finger twitched then tapped against his bed.

*Strange. Hard. Metallic? Dull sounding.*

He tapped again.

*Firm. Solid, yet resonating.*

He opened his hand and laid it flat on the bed.

*Cool. Smooth. Vibrating?*

His elbow bent as he lifted his hand several inches and dropped it back.

*A thud? Unexpected. Calm. Rest. Darkness.*

Rain startled him as the drops pelted the wooden roof. Then it grew quiet. A minute passed. Rain again assailed against the roof. After a moment, the individual sounds of the raindrops converged to a thump. He tried to sit up but collapsed back when his head hit something solid.

*Musty. Damp. Rain?*

He felt around with his hands.

*What in the world?*

Six inches above and to the sides, he imagined his enclosure measured.

*Enclosed? Blankets?*

Again he heard the rain thump against wood.

He opened his eyes.

*Black.*

He screamed.


He awoke from his dream, in his bed, lying on his back. Jackie, his Jack Russell terrier, licked his face. He felt her jabbing nails briskly moving from one spot to another on his arm and chest.

Lick, lick, lick.

"It's okay, Jackie. Daddy was dreaming. Good girl," he said.

But, it wasn't okay.

Sitting up onto his elbows, he tried to open his eyes, but they wouldn't open. He sat upright, touched his eyes, and gasped as he realized his eyes *were* open but he saw black—no colors, no grays, no indication of shapes or light—only black. Disbelief and shock struck him, then dread.

He palmed his eyes and screamed, "Aaaaahhhhhhhh! Oh God ... Oh Lord ... Jesus help me. Please Lord, help me. HELP ME!"

He heard Jackie's nails tick against the wood floor when she jumped off his bed and click along the boards as she ran. Gasping, he placed his feet onto the floor. He fought to calm himself but panicked.

"Noooooo! Noooooo! Noooooooooooo!"

He held the last yell until his breath gave out, and gulped a deep breath of air to prevent his fainting.

He shut his lids and rubbed his eyes until they squeezed back in their sockets, hearing the squeaky sounds inside his head from their rubbing against flesh, eyes against muscle and tendon. He opened his eyes, expecting to see white or red for a minute before his vision returned.

"Daaaammmmmnnnn!"

He rocked forward and back.

"Oh, God. Oh, God. Oh, God..."

He was sure his sight was going to return in any moment.

"Oh, God. Oh, God..." Any moment.

*My phone*, he thought. *Where is my phone?*

He leaned over his nightstand and felt around the objects on it for his cell phone.

"Where is it?" he cried.

Lamp. Clock. Bible. Tablet. Oxygen tube and nasal cannula. No phone.

*Where did I leave it?* he asked himself. *Where the hell is it?*

"Oh, God, help me. Help me. Help me."

He scurried to the nightstand on the opposite side of his bed. Feeling around, he knocked over his pill bottles, one falling to the floor and sounding like a baby's rattle.

No cell phone.

"Daaaammmmmnnnn! Daaaammmmmnnnn!"

He coughed—hard, rasping coughs. His lungs twinged, and he sat back against the pillows for a minute until the coughing stopped.

"I can't see. Jesus Christ, I can't see. Jesus Christ." His words were barely audible.

"Jackie! Here, Jackie. Come to Daddy, baby."

Again he heard her nails clicking across the floor and then felt a small bounce on his bed.

"Jackie. Jackie. Daddy is in trouble." He tilted his face forward, and she licked it avidly.

He reached for the nightstand. On it he felt for the miniature Pieta, the statuette he bought for his grandmother when he was a teenager with his paper route money, a week's pay, after seeing it in the window of the floral shop next to his church. He had carried the figurine for half a mile, worried about dropping and breaking it.

Feeling the sculpture, he grabbed the rosary hanging around its neck, his grandmother's rosary. Clutching the beads, he pulled them to his chest. He felt for the crucifix and grasped it. The cross's corners pierced his palm.

"Hail Mary, full of grace. The Lord is with thee. Blessed art thou amongst women, and blessed is the fruit of thy womb, Jesus. Holy Mary, Mother of God, pray for us sinners, now and at the hour of our death. Amen. Hail Mary, full of grace…"

For ten minutes, he rocked on the edge of his bed while he repeated the prayer, but the darkness remained.

He heard a noise, a scraping sound, which sounded like one of his chairs dragging along the tile floor in his kitchen. The sound lasted for only a second. He froze, listening. The house was quiet.

He began to huff, then to cough again. "Oh God…*Cough*… Oh God…*Coughing*…Oh God."

*Scrape!*

Again the scraping sound came from the kitchen just beyond his bedroom door.

"Who's there?" he called. "Is someone there?"

*Cough! Cough!*

He heard a bumping sound and another scrape, but it was different this time, lower in tone, as if someone bumped into his kitchen table and caused its legs to drag a few inches. Goose pimples rose all over him. His forceful exhalations flexed the tensed hairs on his forearms.

"Someone is there!" he yelled. "I need help. I can't see."

He felt the vibration as Jackie jumped off his bed, and heard her nails clicking and then scratching along the floorboards as she scampered under his bed.

A moment later, he heard pattering on the kitchen floor and growling under his bed. He was confused. How could Jackie be scurrying across the tile floor *and* be growling under his bed at the same time? She couldn't.

*Something got in.*

Imagining an animal had gotten into his house, and wanting his feet off the floor, he jumped to his knees on the bed.

Various animals roved his land, so it was possible that an animal had crawled through the doggy door: an opossum, a raccoon, a bobcat, a fox. Even wolves, bears, and mountain lions roamed this area of Kern County, though it was unlikely a big animal had gotten in. Most likely a squirrel sneaked in. The trees near the house shook with them, and Jackie loved chasing them around the yard, but if a squirrel was in the house, she would have barked her *I'm-gonna-get-you* bark, the one that smacked of frustration from never having caught one of the bushy-tailed rats.

*Right?*

She would've barked and chased a squirrel throughout the house, right?

*It's not a squirrel*, he thought. *Then what in the good name of God is it?*

"Who's there? I know someone is there."

The bedroom door squeaked. He heard the same annoying, yet now petrifying, sound that he had heard for the past three years, since he moved into this small farmhouse off the beaten path—his grandmother's farmhouse. He gasped.

Even while frightened, he thought he should have silenced the irritating door years ago, squirted a little oil into its old hinges.

Then Jackie growled. It wasn't an aggressive or warning growl but was instead a higher-toned one of fear, seeming to say, *"Don't hurt me!"*

He shivered from his own chilling fear.

"Jackie. Here Jackie. Come here, girl," he said with a stressed and jagged tone in his voice. He awaited the clicking of her nails and the bounce of her jump onto his bed. They didn't come, but more growls and woofs did. She sounded scared.

"Jackie. Jackie. Come here. Here."

The door squeaked again. He flinched.

He thought he would wet himself, his undershorts, all he was wearing, the only protection he had between himself and whatever was in the house. He shuffled back, banging his back against the headboard, pinning his chin to his chest and raising his hand out in front of his face.

"Please, I don't want any trouble. I can't see. I need help," he said, not knowing for sure if anyone was in his home, yet unwilling to ignore the possibility that a person had broken in while he had slept, while he was coincidently, and for whatever unknown reason, blind.

Another noise resounded through the room and boomed in his head like an explosion, knocking him again back into the headboard. It wasn't the squeak of his bedroom door but was another recognized sound: the dull, long groan of the boards of his bedroom floor.

"Someone *is* there!" he cried, groping the wall behind him as if seeking to find a hole to crawl through and hide like a rat.

"Get em, Jackie! Get em!" he cried, thinking she would attack whatever or whoever it was, let him know if the person or thing was actually in the bedroom.

She barked several times but stopped when another noise from the floorboards confirmed a *presence*. This time the sound was more of a creak than a groan, as if the weight had entered farther into the room, where the boards sounded at a higher pitch when stepped on—by a person.

Blind and alone with something, possibly someone, in the house, he swallowed hard and his chin quaked. As an adult, he had never been this afraid.

"I'm a God-fearing man!" he yelled, as if the words had protective powers, had protected others from what *bad men* do.

*Creeeak!*

"I pray!" he cried, spurting out another protective incantation from his trembling lips.

*Creeeak! Creeeak!*

The sounds came closer.

His hearing felt more sensitive, more focused, more needed than any other time.

"LEAVE ME ALONE!" he screamed, hurting his throat.

*Creeeak!*

Again it echoed through the room. He heard the boards creak as a weight pushed them down, and creak again when the pressure lifted.

"I have money...Yes, I have lots of money...You can have it...Just get me help...Please!"

Now these words had power, have stopped *bad men* from doing bad things. Oh, yes, these statements would stop the creaking and cause whomever to speak.

Huffing and sweating, he bent over—his head toward his knees, his hands on top of his head, arms protecting his face— and prayed.

"Oh, God, help me. Please, help me. Help me. Help me. Help me."

Without warning, Jackie attacked. At least it sounded as if she did, for she ran out from under the bed, barking and growling, her nails slipping and scratching against the floor. This scared him even more because he had never heard her so upset, so angry, so protective.

Her attack didn't last long.

*"Errt!"* she yipped.

Her assault had failed, by the sound of her nails scurrying on the floorboards and then the tiles in the kitchen and away, likely out the doggy door.

*"Don't hurt my dog, you bastard!"* he fumed. *"Not my dog!"*

He was kneeling straight up in his bed, awaiting a bat to his head, breathing as laboriously as a fish out of water, gulping the air more than inhaling it.

Nothing hit him.

With dripping sweat stinging his eyes, his heart pounding, he waited as the longest two minutes of his life passed.

He tried to recall the creaks in his mind's ear. Had the last creak gone away from him, back toward the door? Did his screams scare away the animal?

He doubted himself. He knew he wasn't dreaming. But was he really blind? Could all light have disappeared, the sun have extinguished, all electricity for lights have stopped? Could he be seeing what couldn't be seen because there was no light by which to see? Was he hearing things that weren't there? He had heard the scrapes and clicks on the tiles, had heard his bedroom door squeak.

A preposterous thought erupted in his mind.

*Am I in my own bed, in my house?*

Of course he was. Jackie was there. He recognized the sounds of her nails hitting the floors, the squeaky hinges of his bedroom door, and the creaking floorboards in his room. His soft bed felt right, and the nightstands and the things on them. He smelled the Chilean sea bass he had fried for dinner, a buttery yet musky odor, which usually filled the house and lingered for a day when he cooked it.

*Maybe it is a large animal.*

He was less afraid of a bear or a mountain lion tearing him apart or even eating him than what a person could do, what people have done.

Still he waited, struggling to control his breathing, to not make the inhaled and exhaled air hiss past his nose. After several tries, he found it quieter to breathe through his mouth.

Hearing nothing in the room, he listened harder for noise beyond his bedroom. He heard his refrigerator's compressor.

*So there is electricity. There should be lights.*

His damn tinnitus was also in his ears. Usually unnoticed, it rang as annoyingly and unwanted as a fire alarm.

He interlaced his hands into a praying position, feeling his slimy palms sliding against each other. He felt the breathed air cool the roof of his mouth. Several small rivulets of sweat ran down his head.

*God help me.*

Again he thought that his mind was perhaps getting the best of him, that he only imagined the sounds and—

He heard something.

*I imagined it.*

He heard it again.

He stiffened, holding his breath.

Again he heard it.

He gasped.

The sound *was* there. But what was he hearing? What was in his room?

He thought it was possibly a muffled and long sigh, an exhalation of air, but he didn't recognize it. Somehow it didn't sound natural, not from an animal or a person.

There it was again. The strange sound was recurring about ten seconds apart. He thought it might be the sound of breathing except the interval between the breaths was longer than usual, longer than his memories thought normal or expected.

*Huuuhhh!*

*Huuuhhh!*

As if exhaling into cupped hands or a cardboard tube.

An image of a gas mask then formed in his mind. It sounded as if someone was breathing through a respirator.

*Someone* is *here.*

Realizing it wasn't an animal in his room, he yelled, "Get out of here! Leave me alone!" and jumped from his bed and lunged to his left to get to his closet. He shoved the door inward and dove into the enclosure. The doorknob banged against the wall. He slammed the door closed and braced his shoulder against it, expecting someone, possibly more than one, or something, to bash into the door.

Believing anyone of significant strength or size could smash his or her way into the closet, he panted, striving not to freak out, to scream or bang or cry, or rush out of the compartment to face God knows what.

The bashing in of the door didn't come, not yet.

Petrified, not knowing what would happen, he considered screaming for help but decided it was a rash idea, a useless waste of energy and perhaps something that could anger whoever, or whatever, was stalking him.

"Oh, Jesus Christ! Jesus Christ. Help me, Jesus. Help me. Help me. Help me, Jesus."

Scenes of similar events in movies ran through his mind. He supposed someone could pierce the door with a knife, sword, or whatnot and stab him. He dropped to the floor, turned onto his back and pressed his feet against the door. Struggling to brace it closed, he reached out for the opposite wall.

"Shit. Shit. Shit."

The closet was too long. He couldn't touch the wall.

Not wanting to get his heels cut or his calves stabbed by something thrust through the space under the door, he raised his feet a few inches off the floor but kept them pressed against the door.

*"I'm blind you stupid bastard!"* he screamed. *"I can't see!"*

His fear was turning to anger.

*Block the door.*

He sprang to his feet, keeping one hand and his weight pressed against the door, and grabbed the wooden rod that held hangers of suits and shirts. It was the length of the enclosure and could be jammed between the door and the opposite wall.

He lifted the end closest to the door off its bracket and pulled to release the other end. The rod and the hangers it held collapsed to the floor. Kicking shirts and suits aside, he forced the rod against the base of the door and moved its other end in front of the opposite wall. But the rod was several inches too short. He began recalling what else he stored in the closet, what he could shove between the end of the rod and the wall. He felt around and found:

Shoeboxes.

*No.*

Shoes.

*No.*

Guitar case.

*What else?*

Old briefcase.

*Yes.*

He placed the case against the wall and pushed the end of the rod against it. A gap remained.

*A shoe.*

He grabbed one and crammed its heel between the case and rod. Tighter, but not perfect, the brace would at least provide him a little protection and time to think.

*What now?*

He was trapped, a blind man in a cave.

*Stand still...Listen.*

If he stayed motionless and quiet, whoever or whatever might leave, so he thought.

He listened desperately.

For several minutes, everything was quiet.

*Just stay still. Focus.*

Nothing happened.

*How long have I been in here?*

He guessed nearly ten minutes had ticked by. What could it be doing? What did it want? What was it?

*Crack!*

He cringed. Having stepped on the suits and shirts, a wooden hanger had snapped. He took another step, and another one cracked.

*The gun!*

He remembered it was leaning in the corner, the twelve-gauge he had purchased twenty-two years ago, just after graduating from the University of California at Los Angeles, when he lived in Encino, where break-ins were common and home invasions a real possibility in the San Fernando Valley—Sad-For-You Valley he had called it.

He had placed the black, ugly thing in the closet to keep it away from visitors and himself. Gun accidents happen he had thought, and yet he had still wanted it close by in case of an emergency, especially if he was sleeping. He could jump out of bed and retrieve the—

*Shells!*

As he reached for the gun, sure it was in the corner—and it was—he remembered that it was empty. He kept the shotgun shells in the drawer of his nightstand. He had thought that in an emergency he could remove the shells from the drawer and then grab the gun from the closet and load it. The procedure would take a minute, but he had figured that it was safer than having a loaded weapon in the open or stowed in the closet. He had figured wrong, since it was now proving not to be safer to have kept it unloaded, or for that matter, to have kept it in the closet.

*If I only had it by the bed. Loaded.*

At least he now had a weapon in his hands. He couldn't shoot it, but it was heavy and made a formidable club, a good head basher.

He got an idea. Grabbing and pulling back on the pump handle, he cycled the gun's action, making the clanking and metal-scraping sounds that pump-action shotguns make, and that most people recognize and fear.

*"I have a gun in here!"* he yelled.

Expecting to hear talking or knocking, maybe banging, a door slamming, or any noise to confirm an intruder and justify his fear, he heard nothing, no one.

He turned the gun around and gripped the end of the barrel with both hands as if it were a bat.

Anticipating someone or something to kick in the door, he was ready to put his adrenaline to work, to fight or flee, if he could. His mind reeled with what could happen: imagining a fist, foot or ax breaking through the door, fighting, being stabbed or shot, and even killed.

*Oh God.*

Twenty minutes seemed to pass. He kept silent. It was hot and stuffy. He was sweating more from emotion than heat. Taking a shirt from the floor, he wiped his face and neck.

Still he waited, for over an hour he believed.

*What time is it?*

He recalled going to bed around eleven, after taking his medications and saying his prayers—to God, to Jesus, to saints, and even Michael and Gabriel—faithful that someone or something would help him, and then awakening blind. And for all he knew, it could have been the same night that he had gone to sleep or the following morning. But regardless of the time, he had to think of something, to do something, to get out of the house, get himself help.

*I can't stay here.*

He contemplated opening the door, rushing to the nightstand and getting the shells, and calculated how long it would take:

To open the door and race the six steps to the nightstand, *three seconds.*

To open the drawer and find at least one shell, *two seconds.*

To load a round, *two seconds.*

And to pump the handle, *one second.*

Then what? Shoot at what? He wouldn't be able see what he was firing at, wouldn't know *what* he was firing at.

What if it was waiting just outside the door? Possibly with a weapon? What would it do, especially when it saw him with the gun, retrieve the shells, and load the magazine? It would certainly protect itself, even if that meant harming or killing. Of course, it would, *right?* Survival of the fittest.

*Too risky. Wait.*

*My phone!*

Where was his phone? He knew he had placed it onto the nightstand as he always did.

He shook his head in disbelief and pushed back his sweaty hair with his hand.

*What the hell is this?*

He felt it on the back of his head where the neck and the base of the skull meet.

*A button.*

He thought a jacket button had stuck to his head when he was on his back and scrambling on the floor.

*What the?*

It didn't peel off. It was round, about the size of a quarter, but the damned thing stayed stuck in his head. It didn't hurt. Hell, he had had no idea the thing was even there.

*A large tack? A nail?*

Had he fallen onto something during the commotion?

He tried to dig the tips of his fingers under its edges and pull harder.

*"Ow!"* It hurt like a son of a bitch as he yanked. He released it, wondering what in the world it was. Somehow his head had banged against the object, or someone had implanted it—

*While I was sleeping? That's impossible!*

He remembered leaving the doctor's office with the fatal news that the cancer had spread in his lungs and that there was no cure—Mesothelioma was lethal even in middle-aged men. Needing to take a walk and wanting to be around people, he stopped at the mall on his way home and bought chocolate truffles for dessert. He cooked himself one of his favorite dinners when he got home: Chilean sea bass with quinoa and sugar snap peas. Lying on his bed before bedtime, he read from a novel and then his Bible, the Bible that his grandmother left in this house she willed to him, the house she had been born and raised in. Then just before sleep—after taking the several medications his doctor prescribed, a handful of pills—he prayed, on his knees, crying like a sick child, pitying himself, afraid of dying, particularly alone, and of having terrifying dreams, especially his most dreadful nightmare: the one in which he is sleeping on his back in his bed when he is awoke by a rush of water and finds himself looking up, while unable to move, through twelve feet of water, water to the ceiling, and he must breathe but knows he cannot, knows he will not get air, and will die alone.

*Then when did this thing get into my head? How did it get into my head? What the hell is it?*

Confusion and fear and disbelief and shock fought for priority in his mind.

Hearing a noise, he jerked. He focused and heard clicking, the familiar sound of Jackie trotting across his floors, and then scratching against the closet door.

"Jackie! It that you, baby?"

More scratching and acknowledging barks.

"Jackie. You okay? You okay? Good girl, Jackie. Good girl. Daddy loves you."

"Ruff. Ruff. Ruff." Scratching.

"Shush…Shush…Sit…Sit…Quiet girl."

She stopped scratching but whined.

He could still hear intermittent little taps, her impatient beating with her front paws up and down on the floor.

"Good girl. Good girl."

More taps and a whine.

*Now what?*

"Ruff."

*Tap! Tap! Tap!*

*What do I do? What the hell do I do?*

"Get your toy. Where's your toy?"

*Tap...Tap! Tap!*

"Ruff. Ruff," she barked, high pitched and excited.

"Get your toy...Beat it up."

He heard her race across the floor, the clicking of her nails getting fainter, going to the small doggy bed in the living room, he imagined, where he kept her toys. She would bring one back and *beat it up*, beat it up if nothing was around, nothing frightening, *nobody* frightening.

A minute later, he again heard the clicking. It got louder until it was again on the other side of the door.

"Beat it up. Beat it up."

She did.

*Thud, thud, thud, thud* in rapid succession.

"Grrrr."

*Thud...Thud! Thud! Thud! Thud! Thud!*

In his mind's eye, he saw her grab her small brown bear by the ear and whip the toy from side to side, onto the floor, trying to break its neck, as she so often did.

"Good girl. Good girl."

"Ruff...Ruff. Ruff."

"Sit. Sit."

*Tap! Tap! Tap!*

She panted, *heh-heh-heh-heh*.

"Good girl. Sit."

He listened and heard nothing strange. Putting his ear to the door, he still heard nothing unusual. He moved over and pressed his ear to the wall. A droning hum, though faint, resonated in his ear.

*The compressor.*

He took in a deep breath and held it, listening for any creak, squeak, or strange breathing sounds. He heard his heartbeat, felt his heart thump against his chest, felt the pulse in his neck and temples. He let the breath out, further drying his mouth.

Several minutes passed. He was sure he would hear something odd, something other than his own heartbeat, but he didn't.

*Nothing...but the compressor...and the tinnitus.*

Harder against the wall he forced his ear, straining his senses, feeling for the feeblest vibration, smelling the bittersweet odor of the naphthalene mothballs he had spread in the closet, and listening for the slightest noise. He heard his stomach growl.

He couldn't be sure nobody or "no thing" was in the house, but he couldn't stay there. He needed a hospital.

Lifting his hand in front of his face, he tried to see it, moved it closer, but still he saw only black. He wondered if he was seeing darkness in the closet or nothing because he was blind.

*The doctors never mentioned blindness.*

Worrying about his eyes, knowing he needed a doctor for them and for "the spike," or whatever it was that was lodged in his head, he decided to open the door.

*I have to get out of here.*

Fighting to build up courage to face the unknown, he inhaled deeply, letting the air out slowly and audibly with his cheeks puffed out.

Again he stepped on a hanger and clothing. It reminded him that he was nearly naked. Rummaging through the clothes on the floor, he found pants, a dress shirt, and wingtips. He put them on, the shoes over his bare feet, rolling up the shirtsleeves. He was ready.

He considered calling out to whoever or whatever was possibly on the other side of the door that he was coming out, but he figured against it.

*No need to rouse it, provoke it, or call it back.*

"Forgive us our trespasses as we forgive those who trespass against us, and lead us not into temptation, but deliver us from evil," he whispered.

Gently, attempting to be quiet, he removed the end of the rod from the door. He was pressing the door closed with his left hand and gripping the rod with his right.

He waited, listening, as a minute passed and nothing unusual happened.

Then he eased the pressure he was applying to the door, keeping his hand up, prepared to push again. Still nothing happened.

So he let go the rod and picked up the gun, holding its barrel awkwardly with his right hand, balancing it like a club. He stood there ready to fight.

Grasping the doorknob with his left hand, he turned it gently and paused for another moment before moving his body back and away from the door. He pulled the door open about an inch, not even revealing a gap between the door and the jamb. Still nothing.

"Jackie," he whispered.

*Tap! Tap! Tap!*

Panting.

"Good girl," he whispered, and pulled the door another few inches and stopped.

He heard her nails striking the floor and felt her nosing his leg.

"It's okay, girl. Sit. Sit."

She stopped nudging but bounced her paws on the floor, making those subtle clicking noises, and panted.

He figured he was as vulnerable as a blind man could be in his predicament, so pushing against the clothing and shoes, he opened the door wide enough to squeeze himself through the space.

*Do or die time.*

Stepping out from the closet, he felt his skin tingle as it entered the cooler space. Nostrils flaring, he inhaled deeply the more oxygenated air. His mind felt clearer, refreshed, quicker. He took several steps toward his bed, wanting to find his phone to get help, hoping he could dial while blind.

Jackie yelped and started shrieking as if she caught her paw in a trap. They were struggling, fear-driven, blood-stopping cries. He heard her. He understood.

*"Jackie! Jackie!"*

He lunged toward her cries, toward the bedroom door.

*"You mother fucker! Let go of my baby!"*

She stopped screaming. He heard her nails click across the floor and out of his room. But it was too late for him to stop. He was in protecting-parent mode, momma-bear mode, attacking forward, swinging the gun wildly, like a crazy man aiming to strike a pinata. He swung back and forth and hit the wall several times, once hitting the doorjamb, causing his hands to sting in pain, but it didn't stop him because he would die before allowing anything or anyone to hurt his baby.

*"Nobody hurts my dog!"*

In his condition, his attack was impressive, continuing for over a minute while he yelled and screamed.

*"Ahhhh! Ahhhh! Bastard!..."*

But it couldn't last much longer. His lungs cramped and his heart clenched, but he continued to swing and gasp and struggle for a gulp of air before he collapsed to the floor.

"Jackie...Jackie...Daddy loves you, Jackie."

He knew he was dying, and he didn't mind going this way, in hot blood, protecting his loved one, facing the unknown like a courageous soldier.

"Just don't hurt my dog," he murmured. "Not my dog."

"Ah!" He wriggled away from the pain—a prick to his arm—and hit the wall, hugging the gun as if it were a rescue buoy. Or was it a sting...or a needle? He breathed strenuously. His mind grew fuzzy, not knowing what to think, what to do, what to say.

Wheezing, he waited. For what, he didn't know. But after a few minutes, he was able to breathe a little easier.

"Who are you!" he finally said as calmly as he could, though it came out as a suppressed yell, mostly exhaled breath.

He attempted to swing the gun in the air. "What do you want?"

No answer.

He struggled to sit up, reached for the nightstand's drawer, pulled it out, and rummaged in it with his hand for a shell.

He found one and fumbled to load it into the magazine.

*"Shit!"*

It fell.

*HUUUHHH!*

No denying it this time. It was loud and close and followed by the sounds of the floorboards.

*Creeeak...Creeeak!*

He gripped the gun, ready to hit a homer. "Don't come closer! I'm warning you!"

*Huuuhhh!*

"What the hell do you want?...What?...I can't see!" he cried.

*Thump! Thump! Thump!*

He felt the bangs on the floor.

He gasped and flinched. He was emotionally and physically drained.

Then the trembling started, beginning with his hands and hastening up his arms and to his shoulders; then his knees quivered and his thighs. The shaking was overwhelming. He dropped the gun and rolled onto his side, into a fetal position—his knees up and together, head tilted forward, elbows together, and hands over his ears as if to block out another of his senses—and sobbed uncontrollably, loudly, sadly, and pitifully; that dynamic blubbering that hits every man once or twice in his lifetime, that I-don't-care-what-happens-to-me-now, life-is-over, I-just-want-to-die bawling. He heaved, choked, coughed, and shook for over ten minutes before he keeled over onto his back, exhausted, defeated, and accepting.

The floor was cool and sucking the last bit of heat and life from his body. He breathed feebly.

Then it was there. It was warm and light, and it stayed... on his arm...and didn't move.

*It's touching me.*

*Huuuhhh...Huuuhhh...Huuuhhh!*

"What? What do you want?" he stammered.

Two thumping sounds came from the floor next to him.

"Didn't you hear me? What?"

Three thumps.

"Yes?"

Three thumps.

"You understand me?"

Three thumps.

Then a flood of memories deluged his mind. He was again a child in this house, playing the game his grandmother had played with him. The game that had finally scared him, had caused him to hide and cower in the hall closet: the *Ouija* board.

*"Don't be afraid, Justin," she had said. "There are no ghosts here, no one to hurt you. They are friends. My friends."*

*"It moved! It moved by itself. I saw it,"* he had told her through the closet door.

*"They're Grandma's friends...your friends."*

He felt another prick, or sting, or needle to his arm.

*It's a needle.*

---

He opened his eyes. He could see. Sunlight seeped through the window curtain in his bedroom. He was lying in his bed. Tilting his head up, he saw Jackie lying next to his thigh, her head resting on his hip, her caring eyes looking into his.

"Jackie!"

She went crazy, jumping onto his chest, then licking his neck and chin and lips.

"Yes, I know. Daddy loves you too. Okay. Okay. Stop. Stop!"

She didn't.

He sat up gingerly, what happened to him flashing in his mind. Though he couldn't recall what occurred after he was stuck with the needle.

*I must have passed out.*

He looked around and saw the gashes in the wall, from where he had hit it with the gun, and the gun lying on the floor. Then he saw something else, something weird, something he hadn't seen since he was twelve. He gasped.

Lying on his bedroom floor was the board, *the* Ouija board, his *grandmother's* Ouija board, the one he and she used to play with, if play it really was. He was sure of it.

*"Who are you?" he had asked the board one late evening after his grandmother had gone to bed. He waited for an answer, for the paddle-shaped planchette to move and point to the black capital letters on the wooden board, the one his grandmother's grandmother had given to her—in 1891.*

*He asked the question again. No answer came. He removed his index finger from the wooden planchette.*

"Aah!"

*He leapt away from the board. The planchette had shifted an inch and stopped. Breathing hard, he stared at it for over a minute, unsure that he saw what he thought he saw. He crept closer, and the wooden paddle moved. He watched as its pointer glided from black letter to black letter, to the letters* G-U-A-R-D-I-A-N-S, *then stopped.*

Angels, *he had thought.* They're angels.

*He asked a second question.* "Where are you from?"

*Again he waited, his eyes fixated on the planchette and his mouth agape, laboring not to make a sound as he exhaled.*

*And it moved, again sliding over the board and pointing to letters before it stopped.*

F-A-R.

*He waited for more letters. . .letters that didn't come.*

Far? Far? *he thought.* Heaven is far. Guardians from heaven.

"Justin!"

*His grandmother's yell startled him. She had walked into the living room while he was playing.*

*"No Justin." she said. "Never without me. Never alone...Not yet."*

Surprised, he covered his mouth with his hand and noticed an even stranger thing: the stubble on his face that he didn't have when he was in the closet—a two-day beard he guessed.

Remembering "the implant" imbedded in his head, he felt behind his head for it. It was gone. The skin and muscle it pierced was swollen, tender, and painful.

He reached for his pills on the nightstand, the anti-inflammatories and pain pills in particular, but the bottles were gone. He looked on the floor, but they weren't there either. The oxygen canister that was between his bed and the nightstand was also missing.

*What the—?*

A thought came to his mind: *The guardians.*

Was it possible?

*Could they be real...Could they be here?*

He closed his eyes, nodded his head, and smiled.

*"Yes."*

He didn't know what *they* did to him or why *they* did it, but he knew at least one thing for certain: his prayers had been answered, he would be okay.

He drew in a breath of air, of relief, and blew it out slowly. Tears blurred his vision.

"Thank you," he said, sure that somehow someone or something heard him.

"So that's all you're going to tell me, that God sent you a guardian angel?" Justin's doctor said.

Turning his palms up, Justin shrugged. "I'm sorry. That's all I can tell you."

"A miracle happens, and you can't tell me how?"

"I told you how."

"Yeah, you prayed about it. I got that."

"I did."

"Well...thank God for you it happened. But you haven't heard the last of this from me. I'll get the answers sooner or later. Expect that."

Justin smiled.

"Yeah, you smile. I want to see you again in two weeks. Two weeks. And call me if anything changes."

"Is that all?"

"Yes, that's all. See the receptionist on the way out."

Justin opened the exam room door to leave. He knew he wouldn't keep the appointment. He didn't have to. He was healthy. He had a *friend*.

# No More Time

A SINGLE LAMP casts a gloomy, yellow haze in our bedroom as I stare at the clock. It is late, and time is long and slow and weighing on me. She will come home around dawn, smelling of booze and sex, and she will understand why I did it. I guess what her reaction will be.

I pick up the gun—it is cold and heavy—and I tremble to rest it against my head. I cry, knowing the last thing I will hear will be my sobbing, and the last thing I will feel will be my tears dripping down my face. To myself, I say, "Good-bye."

# HOW HE FELT AT
# THE COFFEE SHOP

THE COFFEE SHOP was down in the courtyard below street level with its own staircase and entrance from the sidewalk above. As Albert descended the stairs a little after one o'clock in the afternoon, he looked for his reflection in the windows in the door as he always did, expecting them to mirror the white shirt and tie he wore. There was something comfortable and expected about seeing his reflection: the building seemed to welcome him. He didn't see his reflection. Perhaps the light was just not right for it.

As he opened the door, the smell hit him. The scent wasn't what he expected, had remembered, had made him breathe deep and smile: the smell of freshly ground coffee beans—a smell of comfort, safety, familiarity. This time the smell seemed rancid, used, foreboding, and made his upper lip twitch.

Taking the five steps from the doorway to the floor, he imagined himself falling into the cellar. The small ceiling lights piercing the air seemed to be pushing the outside world from the room. The shop was empty but for a young woman tending the bar and a young man sitting in the far corner with a computer and earphones.

Albert sat in a chair at his usual table by the wall facing the street and waited for his wife, Diane, to arrive. He imagined her sauntering over from her Beverly Hills firm just three blocks away, carrying her leather brief bag, the one he gave her when she graduated law school. He thought about how often they used to meet at this coffee shop when he was a pharmaceutical representative and this city was part of his territory. This morning she left for work before he awoke, so he anticipated their talk, wondered how he would feel about her today.

"Can I help you?" the bartender asked.

He turned and looked up at her. She was young and attractive. He didn't know her. The other women he had known were gone.

"No, thank you. I'm waiting for my wife."

She smiled and walked back to the bar.

From the table, he could see up through the high windows to the sidewalk above him. He could see only the legs of the people walking by the building. They, their legs really, just walked by.

The colors of the pants and skirts going by were vivid, so he knew the sun was shining even though he couldn't see it. But he sensed a storm coming, felt tension in the air.

Then he saw her legs descending the stairs. He knew them, and unlike all the other legs that passed by the windows, he knew her face and knew her.

She opened the door and walked in wearing the tight red dress that had always captivated him. Her sculpted body reminded him of the benefits her gym workouts provided: a sexy and desiring image, and a firm and agile body for making love.

But the dress's effect on him was different now. He suffered it. It was appreciated and enjoyed by others. It was used. It was worn. It had been around and flaunted.

She walked over to him. He didn't stand. She kissed his cheek. "Why did we have to meet here?" she asked.

"It's our place," he said.

"It was your place."

"My place."

She didn't sit.

The bartender approached the table. "Can I get you two anything?"

"Do you know what you want?" Diane asked him.

"Hot chocolate," he said, looking at the bartender.

"Are you sure?" Diane asked him.

"I'm sure," he said.

"Just so you're sure," she said.

"In a mug, please, not a paper cup," he said to the bartender.

The bartender nodded and smiled at him, and then she looked at Diane.

"I'll have a latte in a mug," Diane said, and handed the bartender a twenty.

"I'll get it, honey," he said, taking out his credit card.

"What does it matter?" she said, and walked to the back of the room and through the restroom door.

He shook his head and waited.

Five minutes later, Diane returned to the table and took the seat across from him. As she shuffled the chair in closer to the table, the bartender arrived with the drinks. She placed the drinks and the change on the table.

"Here you are," she said. "And your change."

Diane gave her the five-dollar bill that was with the change and said, "Thank you."

"Thanks," the bartender said, then smiled and walked away.

Albert picked up his mug and blew into it.

"When did you get here?" Diane asked.

"Ten minutes before you," he said. Then he placed his mug on the table and stiffened up straight.

"What is it?" she asked. "You got that disgusted look on your face."

"It's got lipstick on it. Someone else was drinking from it."

"Where? Let me see," she said and turned his mug around. "You can barely notice it. It's fine."

"It's tainted. I don't want it. I could get sick, get a disease."

"Here you go again. I can't take this day after day."

"What? I didn't mean anything. It's dirty. That's all."

She looked at him for a moment. "I'll get you another one." She picked up his mug.

"I don't want another one," he said.

"You want this?" she said, brandishing his mug toward him, spilling some of the chocolate onto the table. "Do you want this one?"

"Not anymore. It's no good." He wiped up the spilled chocolate with napkins.

"You're an ass. You know that? A real ass. I'm moving out."

"You say that every day."

"Because you throw this shit at me every day."

She got up and walked to the counter, and spoke with the bartender.

He looked up and saw that the outside world looked different. The brightness was gone. All seemed gray. Then there was a flash and soon a rumble of thunder. He waited. He knew what to expect. The signs were all there. It wasn't long before the rain pelted the ground and its sounds of innumerable cracks and pops filled the room.

Diane soon returned with another mug of hot chocolate for him. "Here. This one isn't tainted." She set it on the table.

He stared at the mug for a minute before picking it up. He held it gently, caressed it with his fingers, felt its smooth, creamy glossiness, how he always did. His mouth opened, and its edges turned down. He let out a sigh of annoyance.

"What now?" she said.

"It's chipped. The lip is chipped." He put the mug on the table.

"It's nothing. Ignore it."

"I can't ignore it. It's not the same. I'm not comfortable with it. It's broken."

"You're doing it again. You have to bring it up, don't you? You just have to. You can't let it go. I can't take this."

"I'm not doing anything. It's cracked. I could cut myself. They shouldn't use it. It needs to be thrown out."

She stood up abruptly, and her leg banged the table. His mug fell to the floor and shattered. The shards scattered, and the liquid spread.

"See what you made me do?" she said.

"I made you do?"

"Bringing up that garbage again."

"I didn't say anything."

"You're an ass."

She hurried to the counter.

He felt the table, remembered how warm and smooth it used to feel on his arms and hands, how he would sit at it and lean against it for hours. Now it was cool and worn. The shellac exterior really just a covering or hiding of a rough and unpleasant looking interior. Seeing through the finish, he saw the grainy and uneven body of the wood. In one place, the protection was worn, cracked, and broken off, revealing the splintered and jagged edges of its core. How is it he ever enjoyed this table, sought it out among the others? Had it been so different, better than the others? He supposed it had always been inferior. He had just overlooked it. Now it didn't have the same importance or nostalgia it once had. He saw it for what it really was. He jerked his hands away from it.

She returned with a few rags to soak up the mess.

"Let me do it," he said, getting to his knees.

"No. Leave me alone. Just leave me alone."

"Hey, you did it, not me."

"What does that mean?" she asked.

"I'm just saying. You did it. I didn't."

"I made a mistake."

"Mistakes."

The bartender came over with a broom and dustpan.

"Please, let me do it. Please," Diane told the bartender.

After hesitating for a moment, the bartender relinquished the broom and dustpan to her and went back to the bar.

Diane placed the large shards in the dustpan with her fingers. "Is this what you want?" she said. "Try drinking out of this. This is broken! This is broken! You can't drink out of this. You'll have nothing, nobody. This is broken."

"All right. All right," he finally said. "I get it. I get it. I'm sorry."

"You're sorry? You're not sorry. You'll do it again tomorrow and the day after that."

"I'm sorry. It won't happen again."

"It better not."

"It won't. I'll stop."

"We'll see," she said, sweeping up the pieces.

He felt ashamed, angry, lonely, and a dozen other emotions he couldn't label but knew they were negative. He had his answer. He knew how he felt about her today. It was how he felt about her yesterday and would feel about her tomorrow.

# BEAUTY ON THE LAWN

SITTING OUTSIDE ON the second floor balcony of our college library, I heard her below on the lawn. I stood and walked to the rail and saw her playing on the grass with a young man. He threw a ball, and she ran and tried to catch it. She ran quickly and turned sharply. She was young, yet an adult, and was blond and sleek and athletic. The man laughed and called out to her. They were having a delightful time under the sunny sky.

I could not keep my eyes off her; she was riveting. I whistled to her—I could not help myself—and she stopped and stared up at me. She seemed to smile but made no sound. I waved to her, but still she did not respond. Then she resumed her play with the man.

I had to get closer to her, so I ran to the first floor and out the back doors and onto the lawn on which the two were playing.

I approached her slowly to see what she would do. She appeared to recognize me as the one who had whistled to her. Dropping her ball, she ran directly toward me, and jumping up at me, she knocked me over. As she and I wrestled, the young man approached us. I asked him if it was okay to play with her. He said it was.

# OUTSIDE HEAVEN'S GATES

I T WAS DARK. Then it was light.

He was walking, but he did not know how long he had been doing so or where he was going, or even where he was. What he did know was that he had to continue to walk. But which way was he going to go? He looked around, but everything looked the same, everything was the same, the same glowing, pearly whiteness that he did not recognize, that he never saw before, that seemed unbelievable. But he was not afraid, even though he could see nothing, nothing near or far, nothing but the pearly whiteness, only the whiteness.

He looked down at his feet. He saw them, and they were his, yes. He felt the control he had over them, and he controlled them to continue to walk, one foot in front of the other, heading for where he did not know but to where he felt compelled to go. And he noticed that his feet stepped on the same whiteness that he saw all about him. Actually, this whiteness was everywhere about him – up, down, right, left—but he did not worry or panic or scream or faint or die. He did not have to. He was where he thought he was supposed to be, where he thought he was expected, where he thought he wanted to be, but he did not know why he thought this.

Then he noticed a golden glint ahead. He walked toward it—for how long, he did not know. Unexpectedly, he found himself approaching an enormous set of golden doors. They were side by side, each appearing to be fifty feet wide, and their height was...He could not see their tops because they were so high. And the sides of the doors were attached to a smooth, tan-colored stone wall that extended beyond his sight to his left and right, and appeared to be as high as the doors.

As he got closer to the doors, he observed a golden desk and someone sitting behind it. He walked right up to the desk and waited, for the large man sitting there—with long, curly, golden-brown hair—was bent over an open book and did not look up.

The man finally raised his head. "You are here, Francis!"

It was then that Francis recalled his name and his memory returned. It was also when he realized that the man sitting at the desk was not like any man he had ever seen. The man had an angelic face of white-marble color. Actually, his face looked as if it *were* white marble, as if he were an ancient Italian statue, carved by one of the great master sculptors.

"Who are you?" Francis asked, staring into the man's sable eyes. "What are you?"

The man stood up, to a height of over seven feet, revealing his coat of golden armor—banded mail of broad horizontal and overlapping strips, covering his massive shoulders and tor-so—forearm guards and greaves, and a sword strapped to his side. Contrasting this golden ensemble was the crimson cape he wore. It was large, extending over a foot past his shoulders on each side and up about a foot over his head, and turning back in toward his body, giving the impression he was standing in front of a backdrop to better reveal his obvious grandeur, size, and probable strength.

"I am Michael," he said with a voice that was loud and resonating.

"Yes, but what are you?"

Michael scowled, his brows pinching together, his lips pulling tight.

"I am the archangel Michael!" he roared, "the defender of heaven, the vanquisher of evil, the slayer of all who defy our God!" With these mighty words that echoed off the wall, the whipping and shearing sounds of fabric pierced the air as his cape burst open and his magnificent silver wings thrust out to his sides and flexed, each and every feather brilliant and perfect, and his right hand drew forth his mighty sword and stabbed it into the sky where lightning struck it and thunder rumbled.

Francis stood fascinated by the immense wings, spreading about fourteen feet from tip to tip, and the silver sword that appeared to shine from within itself. But all this did not frighten him. He spoke calmly, "Where am I?"

Michael retracted his wings, sheathed his sword, and sat back down on the columnar stone stool. "Heaven, of course."

"Heaven?" Francis said. "Where is everyone?"

Michael stared at him for a moment. "They are within the wall."

"Then what am I doing here?" Francis asked, looking around.

Michael shook his head a bit. "You must get past the Doors of Heaven to get into heaven."

"I thought they'd be gates. Shouldn't they be gates?"

"Gates...Doors...You must get past the opening to get into heaven," Michael said.

"Then this, where we are now, isn't heaven?" Francis asked, sweeping his hand out to indicate the surrounding void.

"No, this is heaven too," Michael replied.

Francis looked to both sides of the wall and was amazed by its height and length. "Why does heaven need a wall?"

Michael dropped his gaze and looked down at the book. "I see here you are to be let in."

Francis too looked down at the book but saw nothing on the pages, no words that he could see. "Are you sure?"

"No one has ever entered heaven who did not belong there."

"You said 'there.' You meant 'here,' right?"

Michael's head snapped up, and he glared at Francis, who for a moment saw the angel's dark eyes transform into swirling balls of red flames.

The angel took several deep breaths, if breathing it was, and appeared to force a faint smile. "Just your signature is needed," he said, holding out to Francis a quill that looked to contain no ink. "Just sign your name here," Michael pointed to the book, "and you may enter."

"I have some questions, first," Francis said.

Michael again stood to reveal his full height and splendor. "All your questions will be answered inside."

"That's just it," Francis said. "Why must I wait until I enter the doors? Here is heaven, where I am standing. I have questions now."

"Sign here, and I will answer what questions I can," Michael said, lifting the book and holding it out in front of Francis.

Francis shook his head. "I'd rather not...not before I get some answers."

For the second time, Michael extended his splendid wings while addressing Francis. "You are entering heaven. What else is there to know?"

"Some things just don't make sense," Francis told him.

"What things do not make sense?" Michael asked, retracting his wings and stepping around the desk and coming face to chest with Francis.

"To start with," Francis said, looking up into Michael's face, "where is everyone? Where are the lines of people waiting to get in? There must be thousands to be let in, millions maybe."

Michael paused for a moment. "They have already entered," he said, turning around and walking back behind the desk. "Time does not work the way you imagine it should or recall it being."

"Okay. Then why the need for a wall?"

"It has always been here."

"And why the need for you? A soldier against what?"

Michael flexed his fists as if vexed by the questions. Even his wings jerked slightly.

"Are you going to sign and enter, or not?" he asked.

Looking up, Francis kept his eyes fixed on the black irises looking back at him from their marble frame. "As I said, I'd rather not."

Michael exhaled noisily. "Wait here. Just wait here," he ordered, then turned and walked to the doors. He banged three times on the left one. The golden doors opened outward. Gray mist leaked out, and he entered the opening. The doors closed with a boom.

No sooner had the doors closed, Francis heard what he thought to be powerful horns blowing low, vibrating notes throughout the void. They blew for what seemed to be several minutes until both doors slowly swung open. Then all was quiet.

As the gray mist escaped the opening and spread about as if it were alive and searching for prey, forming long wisps that reached and turned and twisted like large tentacles, he watched anxiously, expecting Michael to return with an army of merciless angels or a pack of ferocious dogs. But a man, or what looked like a man, in a white tunic and wearing a white beard walked confidently out of the opening and over to him. The doors shut with a louder boom than before.

"What is the problem?" the light-skinned man asked.

"Who are you?" Francis asked, noticing the large golden keys hanging from the golden chain around the man's waist.

"I am Peter, holder of the Keys to Heaven," the man said as he expanded his arms and looked around.

"There's no problem," Francis said, looking at the doors and seeing no keyholes, "just questions."

Peter stepped closer to him. "Questions? What questions?"

"Well, now that you ask, more questions come to mind," Francis said, "such as who runs things here? Who's in charge?"

"God, of course."

"What god? Whose god?"

"*The* God. The *only* God," Peter replied, again raising and spreading out his arms.

"And he is?"

"The God of the Bible," Peter said.

"What bible? Whose bible?"

"He is the God of the Jews and Christians. God Almighty."

"So he is the god who is written about in that black Bible people on earth are so familiar with?"

"Yes, yes. Now you understand." Peter smiled.

"I understand what I know about the God of the Bible," Francis said. "That God is a terrible god," he continued. "I fear that God. I don't want to be anywhere near that God. And I don't want to worship anyone, certainly not forever."

"But this is heaven, where everyone wants to be, where all is known."

"I don't think I want to be here," Francis told him. "I don't trust this place or whoever is controlling things here."

"Why do you say that?"

Francis thought for a moment. "Is God anything like what the Bible says He is?"

"Well, that is a complicated question that only God—"

"Yes or no?"

"You don't understand—"

"Yes or no? I understand 'yes' or 'no.'"

"Okay, yes, but—"

"So, that's it. I shouldn't trust this place."

"No, no. That's not what it means."

"Then what does it mean?"

"It means you've rightfully earned a place in heaven, and that place is waiting for you … just behind the wall. The magnificence of heaven awaits you."

"What if I don't want to go in?"

"Not go in?" Peter said. "I don't understand."

"Yes, not go in," Francis said. "What happens to me if I choose not to go in there?" He pointed to the doors.

"Not go in? Not go in?" Peter repeated. "May the saints have mercy, not go in. You're not serious?"

"I am serious. As serious as I have ever been, at least as a… What am I referred to now?"

"An immortal soul," Peter said.

"As an immortal soul," Francis said.

Peter stood still and remained quiet. He looked to be thinking. Finally, he said, "We have never had anyone refuse to enter heaven. We have had billions refused entrance, sent to exist in other places, but never, absolutely never, has anyone not entered the Doors of Heaven when they have been opened to him or her." Peter pointed to the book on the desk. "Everything is in this book."

"So, I would be the first," Francis said.

"Well, no, you wouldn't be the first. It's not allowed."

"Not allowed?"

"Yes, not allowed," Peter repeated.

"Is that in your book?"

Peter did not answer but looked down at the open book and thudded it closed. "It has nothing to do with the book."

"I thought you said *everything* is in that book."

"I did, but that's not what I meant. This is different."

"Different how?"

Peter sighed, and stroked his chin and beard with his fingers. "I must get someone to assist us."

"Who? Who is going to assist us?" Francis asked.

"Remain here. I'll return shortly."

Francis looked around. "Where can I go?"

"More than you know," Peter answered and stepped back towards the colossal doors. They opened just enough to allow him to enter and mist to seep out. Then they closed, again with a resonating boom.

Francis waited. For how long, he did not know, but it seemed to be about ten minutes. He did not know how time worked in heaven. A minute could have been a millennium on earth, or vice versa, for all he knew. He decided to sit. But just as he was about to squat, he heard and saw the magnificent doors again open. And this time they opened wide, all the way, till they reached the wall with a bang that shook the air. He expected to pleasure his eyes and mind with the wonderments of heaven that lay beyond the opening. But it did not happen. What he saw was billowy gray mist that obscured everything beyond the wall, if anything was there. He stared at the opening.

After several minutes, Peter finally stepped out from the mist and strode back to the desk. The doors remained open.

"Someone is coming to assist us," Peter said.

"Assist us? With what? Who is coming?"

"You'll know."

Ideas shot through Francis's mind. Was this 'someone' a he or a she, a man or a woman, angel or prophet, or maybe God himself? Peter remained standing with a stoic face. Then there was noise, loud trumpets blasting a melody that Francis found foreboding—long, low notes. Thunder sounded and the void quaked. A wave of gray mist shot out from the opening and spread. He could see nothing through the thick mist. He was scared for the first time as an immortal soul.

A couple of minutes passed before the mist outside the opening began to die away, and he saw the 'someone' standing just outside the doors: an olive-skinned man, wearing a red tunic. He had long brown hair and a beard. As the man approached the desk, he held up his hand, and Francis could see what looked to be a red wound centered in the man's palm.

Francis's eyes opened wide and his mouth gaped.

"Jesus."

"Yes," Peter said. "He is Jesus."

Jesus walked up to Peter.

"This is the one, Master," Peter said.

Jesus looked at Francis and nodded slightly.

"He doesn't want to enter heaven," Peter said.

"Well, no, that's not exactly correct," Francis said. "It's not that I don't *want* to enter heaven. I want to enter *the* heaven, the one of my dreams, the one I hoped and prayed for, the heaven of wonders and happiness. You know...what humans have come to expect."

Jesus spoke, or at least that 'someone' spoke. "This is heaven."

"Yes, Peter told me, if Peter is your name," Francis said, looking at Peter and back to Jesus. "He told me this is heaven."

"So it is," Jesus said.

"But I can see I was wrong about heaven; it's not as I imagined it."

"I assure you this is heaven," Jesus said.

"Yes, but I have questions," Francis said. "Many questions, actually."

"All your questions will be answered in heaven," Jesus said.

"In heaven?" Francis said.

"Yes, heaven," Jesus said. "Beyond the doors."

"I thought this was heaven," Francis said.

"This is heaven," Jesus said.

"Then I'm already in heaven," Francis said.

"Yes, this is heaven," Jesus repeated.

"Then I would like the answers to my questions now, being I'm in heaven."

"What I meant was your questions will be answered once you enter beyond the doors," Jesus said.

"There! There is a concern I have," Francis said. "Why must I enter beyond the opening? I wish to know the answers to my questions before I decide to enter through that gap in the wall." He pointed to the opening.

Peter whispered something into Jesus' ear. Jesus nodded then turned his attention back to Francis.

"You know who I am," Jesus said to Francis.

"I know who you might be," Francis told him.

"I'm Jesus."

"I guessed that," Francis said.

"So, you can trust me," Jesus said.

"You're telling me you're Jesus, but I don't know if you're *the* Jesus. And if you're the Jesus written and preached about, I still don't know if the stories about you are true."

"What do you desire to know?" Jesus asked Francis.

"Are you the son of God? Are you God?"

"If I said yes, you would still have doubts," Jesus said.

"That's true," Francis said.

"I can work a miracle to prove to you who I am," Jesus said.

"Possibly others can work miracles in heaven," Francis said. "Maybe everyone in heaven can work miracles."

"How dare you!" Peter said, taking an aggressive step toward Francis.

"I dare because I'm here," Francis said. "I should be safe in heaven, free from all pain and suffering, and I should have all my questions answered."

Francis stared into Jesus' eyes, waiting for him to speak. But Jesus placed his hand on Peter's shoulder and walked him about twenty feet away. Francis could not hear their discussion.

They returned after a few minutes.

"Why are you so concerned?" Jesus asked Francis.

"To begin with, if this is heaven, all this around us, why is there a wall and closed doors? Is it to keep whomever or whatever in or out? Why would heaven need to keep anything in or out? It's as if there's a heaven inside heaven that's surrounded by an impenetrable wall. And where are all the people? There should be a very long line here. If I can make it here, most people can."

"You will understand when you are inside."

"What's inside?"

"Heaven."

"Can I look inside?"

"You will see everything from inside."

"No, from here. Can I look from here?"

"No, the mist blocks all sight."

"Yes, but why? What am I not supposed to see? I'm already in heaven, so I should be able to see everything."

Jesus did not answer.

"How about a tour?" Francis asked him. "Can I get a tour of the inside, possibly a trial run, to see if I like what I find?"

"Who would not like heaven?" Jesus said.

"You didn't answer my question."

"No. No you cannot test heaven."

"Must I enter? Will I be forced to enter? I want to know."

"Everyone enters."

"Yes, but is anyone forced? What if someone chooses not to enter?"

"Who would not want to enter heaven?"

"I for one."

"Why?"

"I don't like what I believe I know about God, the God that I learned about, that I read about. And I don't trust a heaven ruled by Him."

Jesus leaned over and whispered to Peter. Then they turned around, continuing to talk. Francis could not make out what they said, but he watched them intently. Peter gestured with his hands while he spoke. Jesus nodded his head intermittently. They spoke for a couple of minutes, before they turned back to face Francis, who remained still and silent, as if awaiting judgment in court.

"What is it you want?" Jesus asked Francis.

Francis did not answer immediately but thought about the question. Did he wish to enter heaven, the real heaven, whatever it was, or did he want to see beyond the doors before deciding? He was unsure, so he made a simple choice, the easiest one he could make with the knowledge he had.

"I want to live," he told them. "I want to live!"

Jesus looked at Peter and nodded. Suddenly they grabbed Francis by the wrists and began pulling him.

"What! What are you doing?" Francis shouted. "Wait! Wait!"

They were dragging him toward the opening in the wall.

"No! Stop! Stop! Please!"

They did not say a word to him.

He saw the mist getting closer.

"No! No! I don't want to go in! I don't want to go in! Stop! Please!"

A few feet from the entrance, a tendril of mist reached out and grabbed him. He could feel its grip. He felt a shove on his back.

"Francis! Francis! Are you all right? Francis!"

Francis heard the voice and opened his eyes.

"Francis, you're alive!"

"Alive?"

"You passed out. You stopped breathing. I thought you were dead."

"I was! I was dead!"

"What?"

"I was in heaven! I asked to live!"

"What?"

"I asked to live!"

"Heaven? Live? We're getting you to a hospital."

# MALE REGRESSION

As the carpool van turned in the street, Helen did not return the waves back to the two workmates who waved to her. As it drove away, leaving her alone, she slowly staggered up the driveway and to the locked side door of her home. With her head down, chin to her chest, she hesitated to knock. She took in several deep breaths. Then raising her hand sluggishly, she let her prominent knuckles strike against the plank. The doorbell would only scare him, she knew.

Anxiously she waited and then knocked again. Still the door did not open, nor did she hear a voice from behind it. There was no ambulance, no cars in the driveway, no items in the yard or by the door to suggest something had happened. She rapped again, unwilling to push the doorbell button.

The voice finally came, as she knew it would, from inside. "Is that you, Helen?" the voice asked.

"Yes," was all Helen said.

She heard the nurse unlocking the several locks she had especially installed on the inside of the door and knew it would take a minute to unbolt them.

The door squeaked open. Angela stood there wearing her white nurse uniform. "He's fine," she told Helen.

"Where is he?" Helen asked.

"He's watching cartoons in your bedroom," Angela said. "Would you like me to get him?"

"No, that's okay. I'm exhausted."

"He gave me little trouble today."

"Did you take him on his walk?" Helen asked, hoping the answer was yes because she was in no mood to take him.

"Yes, around the neighborhood," Angela said.

"No problems?" Helen asked, taking a seat on the sofa.

"Nothing unexpected," Angela said.

Helen, her eyebrows raised, gave Angela a concerned stare and waited timidly for what else she would say.

"We did come across two others being walked." Angela added, then paused for a moment. "When we passed them, he started to yell."

"Oh, my God, he's getting worse," Helen said.

"It wasn't that bad," Angela said. "I told him, 'No!' and he stopped."

Helen gave her a feeble smile and nodded her head.

"And he had another accident this afternoon," Angela said.

Helen rubbed her temple. "Again?"

"I cleaned him up and changed him. It wasn't a big problem. Really, Helen, don't worry about it. It happens. It's normal."

From an end table, Helen picked up a framed picture of him. It was her favorite. A picture of when he was young and strong and himself. She began to cry. "What am I going to do?"

"You'll do what most women do," Angela said, "what you have to do."

Biting her lower lip, tears running down her face, Helen looked up at Angela. "I'm worried about the insurance and paying for you."

Angela nodded her head. "Government insurance will cover me for another month."

Helen looked at her hand and began turning her gold wedding band on her finger. "That's all the time they're giving me?"

"In his condition, that is a long time," Angela said.

"I have savings," Helen said. "I can sell the house."

"Now, Helen, let's not be foolish or sentimental. You can do nothing to help him. He's in the final stage. You would only be wasting your money. You know this. You know this. Come on."

"You're right." Helen said, looking at her wedding picture on the wall. He was so handsome in the picture, she thought. He was still handsome.

"Who are you?" a man's voice said, startling Helen. He was standing in the doorway.

Helen cringed. *Who am I?* she thought. *Who am I? I'm your damn wife. Your damn wife for the past thirty-seven years.*

"Honey, I'm your wife, Helen."

"What honey?" he asked.

"You, Al. I meant you, for God's sake."

"I'm Al," he said.

"I know, dear."

"Where's the deer?"

"No, Al, there is no deer," Helen said, slamming her hand down on the table.

"Calm down, Helen," Angela said. "You know this is the process. This is all normal. The way it is."

"I know, I know," Helen said and began to sob.

"All men go through this regression eventually," Angela said.

"I know, but I can't take much more of this."

"It's almost over. I spoke with the doctors. They said you could put him down any time now. He has lost his ability for abstract thought. He's just...well he's just...you know. He just is."

Helen lifted her head as if she heard something to give her hope. "They said I can put him down? When?"

"Whenever you want," Angela told her.

"Who is going down?" Al asked. "Down what?"

Helen turned and stared at Al. She smiled, tears dripping down her face. "You look good, Al. Real good," she said, seeking to show kindness to the man who was no longer the husband he had been.

Al looked down at his legs and then stuck out his arm and studied it. "I have pants and a shirt," he said.

"It's no use, Helen," Angela said. "Don't get yourself worked up over this. Other women all over the world are experiencing similar interactions with men."

"Yeah, but how long am I supposed to continue to *experience* him?"

"We can bring him to the hospital tomorrow. It can be over tomorrow, Helen." Helen looked into Angela's eyes, trying to register how it would feel to be done with her situation with Al. "Tomorrow?"

"Tomorrow, Helen. You can be free of this tomorrow."

"I can start over?"

"Yes, and there are plenty of young men waiting to be adopted. You can adopt two or three if you like. You could use a new husband or two, right?"

Helen knew she could. *A new husband,* she thought. It sounded good. But she was not sure she would want to go through "male regression" with another man ever again. *That damn Y chromosome.*